MW00531892

Praise For *Under the Eye of the Big Bird*

"No other book of hers convinces me more that Kawakami used to be a teacher of chemistry. A sad but beautiful depiction of a perishing world."
—Banana Yoshimoto

Praise For *People From My Neighborhood*

"*People from My Neighborhood* blooms with life. I loved these distinctive characters and their stories with universal underpinnings of folklore and myth. Reading this book felt like I was on a guided walking tour of a community, led by Kawakami's singular sensibility and elastic range."
—Kali Fajardo-Anstine, author of *Sabrina & Corina*

"No one writes like Hiromi Kawakami. In *People from My Neighborhood*, Kawakami reminds us of what a gift and a rarity it is to read her work. Her characters love, lose, grow, and fall, while Kawakami paints murals of their lives with the deftest of hands. The depth and complexity of these stories is simply beyond, and Kawakami's prose, from cover to cover, couldn't be a bigger joy to live with. It will always be a mystery to me how she pulled it off, but *People from My Neighborhood* is a world unto itself—and we couldn't be luckier to get to read it."
—Bryan Washington, author of *Memorial* and *Lot*

"Beguiling, with a strangeness that feels culturally rooted."
—*The Sunday Times*

"Offers a delicious combination of intrigue, magic and comedy, like an unusual but satisfying snack. Kawakami continues to show off her prowess as a sharp-witted writer with a keen eye for the unexplored mysteries of humanity."
—*The Japan Times*

"Tempting as it is, *People from My Neighborhood* is not a book to rush . . . The interlinking short stories in this collection are fairy tales in the best Brothers Grimm tradition: naïf, magical and frequently veering into the macabre . . . In a world where much is insubstantial . . . Kawakami's clean narrative style is very much her own."
—*Financial Times*

"It would be fair to describe the stories as surreal. But as the pages slid by, I found myself thinking . . . how could I talk about my neighbors without this level of surrealism? I know so little about who they really are. I see their lives in flashes, out of context, on guard and on display. They are the perfect subject for the genre. And what's more, when I was a child, didn't I imagine them as caricatures—witches, old men, seers, rebels, charlatans? It's as though *People from My Neighborhood* reminds us of how we once perceived the world."

—*The Arts Desk*

Praise For *Parade*

"The presentation is exquisite: slightly smaller than a single hand, Kawakami's spare text is interrupted by Takako Yoshitomi's delightful two-color illustrations of mostly geometric shapes with anthropomorphized additions. Subtitled 'A Folktale,' this less-than-100-page tome easily stands alone as a parable about memory, mythic characters, and confessional regrets, but for a lingering, sigh-inducing experience, read this only after finishing its companion, the internationally bestselling, Man Asian Literary Prize finalist, *Strange Weather in Tokyo* . . . An ethereal, resonating literary gift."

—*Booklist* (starred review)

"An atmospheric novella that will delight both devotees as well as newcomers looking for something out of the ordinary."

—Adam Rosenbeck, *International Examiner*

"Brief, haunting." —Esther Allen, *Words Without Borders*

"Regardless of your age, there are moments that elicit childlike joy from the reader . . . A highly enjoyable and soothing read that leaves a lingering sentiment for the reader to reflect upon."

—Daljinder Johal, *Asymptote*

"A moving story of kindness with the subtle and beautiful writing Kawakami's known for and captivating illustrations by Takako Yoshitomi, *Parade* will prove to be a precious keepsake for fans of Kawakami and *Strange Weather in Tokyo*." —Pierce Alquist, *Book Riot*

"Part fairy tale, in which some readers will discern a moral, part gentle reminiscence of childhood's passing miracles and memorable pains, Kawakami's compact novel is gentle, charming and smart, as 'pretty . . . and sad' as the sparkling touches of the tengu." —*Publishers Weekly*

"Enigmatic novella in which the world of Japanese mythology intrudes into the mortal realm . . . Like so much of Kawakami's work, an elegant mystery that questions reality in the most ordinary of situations." —*Kirkus Reviews*

"Here [Kawakami] goes full pelt into fantasy, leaving quirky some ways behind with a tale in which folklore and modernity collide." —Iain Maloney, *The Japan Times*

Praise For *Strange Weather in Tokyo*

"Simply and earnestly told, this is a profound exploration of human connection and the ways love can be found in surprising new places." —*BuzzFeed*

"A sweet and poignant story of love and loneliness . . . A beautiful introductory book to Kawakami's distinct style." —*Book Riot*

"In quiet, nature-infused prose that stresses both characters' solitude, Kawakami subtly captures the cyclic patterns of loneliness while weighing the definition of love." —*Booklist*

"Each chapter of the book is like a haiku, incorporating seasonal references to the moon, mushroom picking and cherry blossoms. The chapters are whimsical and often melancholy, but humor is never far away . . . It is a celebration of friendship, the ordinary and individuality and a rumination on intimacy, love and loneliness." —Japan Society

"A dreamlike spell of a novel, full of humor, sadness, warmth, and tremendous subtlety. I read this in one sitting, and I think it will haunt me for a long time." —Amy Sackville

Also by Hiromi Kawakami

Strange Weather in Tokyo

Manazuru

Parade

People from My Neighborhood

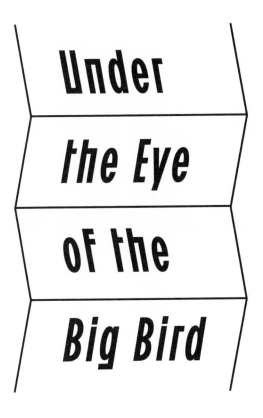

Under the Eye of the Big Bird

A NOVEL

Hiromi Kawakami

Translated from the Japanese by Asa Yoneda

Soft Skull
New York

UNDER THE EYE OF THE BIG BIRD

First Soft Skull edition: 2024

Library of Congress Cataloging-in-Publication Data
Names: Kawakami, Hiromi, 1958- author. | Yoneda, Asa, translator.
Title: Under the eye of the big bird : a novel / Hiromi Kawakami ;
translated from the Japanese by Asa Yoneda.
Other titles: Ōkina tori ni sarawarenaiyō. English
Description: First Soft Skull edition. | New York, NY : Soft Skull Press,
2024.
Identifiers: LCCN 2024011314 | ISBN 9781593766115 (hardcover) | ISBN
9781593766207 (ebook)
Subjects: LCGFT: Science fiction. | Novels.
Classification: LCC PL855.A859 O3713 2024 | DDC 895.63/6—dc23/
eng/20240501
LC record available at https://lccn.loc.gov/2024011314

Jacket design by Farjana Yasmin
Jacket image © iStock / leminuit
Book design by Laura Berry

Soft Skull Press
New York, NY
www.softskull.com

Printed in the United States of America

1 3 5 7 9 10 8 6 4 2

| *Contents* |

| *Keepsakes* |

Let's go to the baths today, Miss Ikuko said, so we all got ready.

In our robes of white gauze, we took the children by their hands, formed a line, and walked the five minutes or so to the river, down the flagstone path. Some of the stones were missing where they had come loose. Up ahead, Miss Chiaki stopped every so often at these empty spots, crouching to scoop up the fragments scattered on the ground into her palm.

"It could be much worse," Miss Ikuko said soothingly.

Miss Chiaki nodded. "You're right. We're fortunate here."

Miss Chiaki gathered her robe around her and continued walking, a little faster now. We could hear the river and see the steam rising through the trees. This was a natural bathing spot.

We sank ourselves into the water and warmed our bodies. Our breasts and pale bellies were visible through our robes. One of us soaked her feet, while another submersed herself all the way up to her neck. We flushed faintly and soon started to perspire.

The children kept together, splashing in a shallow some distance from us. Their voices carried over the surface of the water as they played.

Farther down, an animal was swimming toward the other bank. Miss Chiaki gave a small cough. One of us said, *Is it time we were going?* Still in our robes, we rose out of the pool and made our way back, spilling drops of water. After our homeward procession had passed, the cobblestones shone wetly for some time, as in the wake of a giant snake.

I got married five years ago.

My husband is tall and generously built. I am tall for a woman, but when he hugs me, I feel as though I've been neatly rolled in heavy cloth, which is very pleasant.

My husband commutes to a factory at the edge of the city. Each region has a similar factory, but I have heard a rumor that even among those, this one is of an especially high standard.

Miss Ikuko laughs and says no. "They're all the same. The technology is identical, after all."

But even if the technology and the workings are the same, might not the quality of what is produced differ according to the skill of those working at the factory? I said so to my husband once, and he nodded, seeming pleased.

Several times a week, I think about how much I love my husband. When I notice these feelings I have for him, it makes me feel relieved, and also a little uneasy.

While my husband is at work, I raise children.

The children are full of energy. Miss Ikuko has been mentioning more often recently how it runs her out of breath to keep up. Before, she would be the first one to join in their games.

We take them to play in the big park in the middle of the city.

This park has a fountain and a trickling stream, a climbing frame, a sandbox, and a small carousel. The children are allowed on the carousel once they have entered kindergarten. So in spring, when they first start at kindergarten, they rush to climb astride the wooden horses and show off how they ride around and around. Soon, though, they tire of it, and go back to playing house and tag and kick-the-can.

The carousel attendant is an elderly man. He once told me that he resided somewhere in the north of the city.

By autumn, hardly any children ride the carousel. The attendant sits quietly next to the silent platform. Every once in a while, a child decides to jump onto a wooden horse, and then the attendant pulls a kind of large lever installed next to the platform. Slowly, the platform starts to turn. Tinny music plays. After exactly eight rotations, the platform stops. Underwhelmed, the child gets off the horse, and without a backward glance runs off toward the sandbox.

–

Miss Chiaki has been married three times. Her first husband died two years after they got married, and the next was with her for seven years but then also fell ill and died. She registered her marriage with her current husband last year.

"Why bother making it official?" Miss Ikuko says to me behind Miss Chiaki's back, but I think I understand.

Of course, registering the marriage doesn't change anything. Either way, the two of you live together, and quietly grow older.

"Perhaps she wants to have something to mark the time they spend together," I suggest.

Miss Ikuko laughs and looks askance. "I guess so."

My husband and I have registered our partnership, although he wasn't keen to at first.

"It looks like I might be around for a while," he said.

"And me? You don't think I'll live very long?" I said.

He shrugged. "We don't know, do we? No one can know that."

This is my husband's fourth marriage, and my second. His other wives and my previous husband are all dead. Unlike me, my husband has his wives' keepsakes. He keeps each one in its own small box neatly lined with cotton.

Sometimes I try to remember all the children I've raised so far.

Pito, puta, mita, yota . . . Even counting up just the children whose names I can recall, there are fifteen of them. If

I include the ones I've forgotten, the number must easily be over fifty.

The children grow quickly. It's rare that a child takes as long as two or three years to become ready for kindergarten, and the fast ones can be ready at three months.

Once they enter kindergarten, my work is nearly done. If I were to meet any of those fifteen children now, whose names I remember but who all grew up and left, I don't know that I'd recognize them straightaway.

Recently, I had a visit from someone who must have once been one of those children.

"Hello, Mother?" The child held out a sprig of flowers. They were small white flowers that grow on a hillock near the factory. "I picked these for you," he said shyly.

I hesitated, trying to recall his name.

"It's Taku."

"Yes." He had been . . . not in the first ten, but certainly one of the first twenty or so of the children. "How tall you are!" Out of instinct I reached out and took his hands, and the child gently squeezed back.

"I'm going to be getting married."

"Well!"

"When was I your child?"

"You know I can't tell you that. Just like you're not supposed to come here."

I looked around discreetly, but there was no one there to admonish us. I hadn't seen Miss Ikuko today. I put my arms around his torso and held him tightly. This child I had raised—I could feel the firm warm muscle of him breathing.

"Congratulations," I whispered.

Taku smiled sweetly and lowered his head. Hugging me back, he said, "I'm so glad I came."

Then he left, looking back over his shoulder, seeming sorry to be leaving.

Are things going well at the factory? I ask my husband.

He shrugs his shoulders in a way that can be taken as either *uh-huh* or *nuh-uh*.

They say the factory in this region was built around a hundred years ago. The other regions' factories are around the same age. The very first one was built several hundred years ago, but that one no longer exists. Also, at that time, there was a unit that contained multiple regions, called a *country*, and that *country* was named Japan. And as well as Japan, there were countless other *countries*, each of which had a name. I learned all this from my husband, who enjoys reading old documents.

What was life like back then? I ask him.

He shakes his head. We don't know. It's not recorded anywhere. I expect that's something we're not supposed to know.

There are many things in this world that we aren't supposed to know.

Miss Ikuko once took me aside and said, You're a little inquisitive. That's fine, of course. People ought to have a thirst for knowledge. Life is short, after all.

The factory makes food, and also children.

The origins of the children are randomized. Some are derived from cows; others from whales or rabbits.

"Why don't they make human-derived children?"

"I think there must be a small number made," my husband says. "But the human-derived stem cells are fragile."

"Really?"

"For some reason, cells harvested from people who are human-derived are much more likely to mutate. We don't have a lot of luck using them to produce children."

"Really."

None of us is allowed to know what our animal of origin is. Did the people back then also live in a world with so many things they couldn't know? I wonder.

"Will you show me your keepsakes of your wives?" I ask.

Sure, my husband says, and brings out the boxes.

My husband told me that his first wife had been of mouse origin. The next one was of horse origin, and the third, of kangaroo.

Each box contains a bone, which is the keepsake. For some reason, the small bone called the analogous bone, which is located near the cervical spine, takes on the shape of the skull of the animal a person is derived from—only in miniature, of course. After someone dies, before the body is incinerated and pulverized at the factory, you can put in a request to be given the analogous bone. It's only once someone's dead that we can know what their heritage was.

My favorite is the analogous bone belonging to the

horse-based wife. Its snout sweeps so prettily away from the eye sockets, and it looks as though it might start talking to me at any moment.

"Which wife did you like best?"

"The one I have now."

If I die before my husband, I wonder, will he keep my analogous bone in a fourth box? I'd be happier if he didn't, I think.

"I don't want to end up like your other wives," I say, to see how he'll respond.

He smiles and says, "I agree. Let me think about it."

But then, just like that, my husband was dead.

I put in my request at the factory counter and was given his analogous bone. I went to the library and looked it up in a reference book, which showed me that it closely resembled the skull of a dolphin.

The caption placed next to the photograph of swimming dolphins said: *Dolphin: a generic name for the smaller varieties within Odontoceti, suborder Cetacea, order Cetartiodactyla, class Mammalia.*

For quite some time, I felt like doing nothing at all.

"You mustn't be down for too long, for the children's sakes, too. I'm sure your dead husband would want the same," Miss Ikuko said, trying to be encouraging.

But even the thought of the children didn't appeal to me. "All they make is mess and trouble."

"Don't be silly!" Miss Ikuko raised her voice. "If we

lose the children, that's the end of the world. We have to make the children and raise them, because that's how we maintain the biological diversity of the genetic information we need to preserve. That's the only way the world keeps going."

I have trouble understanding what she's saying. Of course, they're words I've had repeated to me daily, ever since I too was a child. But I don't know what it all means.

"Where did people come from, Miss Chiaki?" I asked.

Would you like to go to the baths, just the two of us? I'd suggested. I was trying to avoid Miss Ikuko.

Miss Chiaki immediately said yes, and the two of us put on our light robes and walked to the river. Miss Chiaki didn't say much. She didn't mention my dead husband or the children, for which I was grateful.

Bubbles formed on the surface of the river. Vapor rose and drifted away. The two of us sat in the water without talking for a long time. Sweat ran down our foreheads and temples and the sides of our necks, but we stayed like that for a while.

It started to get dark. Miss Chiaki quietly got out of the water. Her breasts and her belly were flushed pink.

"Your husband who died the other day," Miss Chiaki said simply. "You loved him."

I nodded. I felt tears trickle down my face. From my eyes and my nose.

"May I show you something?" Miss Chiaki took a flat square tin from the small bag she had left on the bank. She opened the lid and showed me what was inside.

"What is it?"

"The soul of the throat. Some people call it an Adam's apple."

The small bone that lay on the cotton was nothing like an analogous bone: not like a skull at all, but like a butterfly that had failed to open its wings.

"Human-derived people don't have an analogous bone. So they give you the Adam's apple instead, because it's unique to human-derived people.

"When the factory sent me this bone, I was taken aback. I never dreamed my second husband might have been of human heritage. He was pretty old, so I knew it had to be a long-lived mammal, but still." Miss Chiaki smiled gently. "Do you know, they say only three people have ever been derived from humans?"

"What about from other mammals?"

"There must be at least a thousand per species, even the rarest ones. That's what my first husband said."

Miss Chiaki's first husband had been deputy chief at the factory, so it stood to reason that he would have known information like this, which was kept from the rest of us.

"Why are factories always making so many people?"

"Oh, but they make food, too."

Food, meaning things other than people. Animals, plants—they were all made in factories.

"Don't you think there's something strange about the way that we live just to be made and raised, and to marry, and raise children, and then die again?"

"But that's simply how it goes."

Miss Chiaki reached toward a worn flagstone on the path

and stroked it with her fingers. Our skin under our gauzy robes was no longer flushed, but pale and tender.

"This path has been here for a thousand years," Miss Chiaki said.

"Is that really true?"

"My first husband used to say so."

"Who made it?"

"Humans."

"Why?"

"That, I don't know."

I thought about the sand on the bed of the river where we had just bathed. After the bones of the dead are pulverized, they're put in the river. My husband's bones, and eventually my bones, too, will mix with the countless grains of sand and continue to be trodden underfoot by women for years to come.

"She likes the story about the man and the woman who go down the river in a small boat," Miss Ikuko says.

"I would never have guessed."

"I know. I'm not entirely sure why myself."

The man and the woman leave the city and set out in a boat. They're the first ones ever to think of doing this. The boat is swept out to sea, and the man and the woman wash ashore on an unknown continent, where they raise children and build a new city.

"That story's a myth," Miss Chiaki says quietly.

What's a myth?

A story about gods.

What are gods?

I'm not sure, but they must be something like a factory.

The women's talk shifts like ripples on the water.

They had children, so I guess there must have been facto-ries on that continent, too.

I bet they're nothing like ours.

Wouldn't you like to see them?

But I'd be too afraid to go down the river.

There are shouts from the children. One of the bigger ones is playing at drowning. You mustn't, Miss Ikuko scolds. What if you really do drown?

A long-eared animal is swimming near the other bank. It's a kind of animal normally used for food, but the ones that break free and get across the river are able to escape being eaten.

Do you think that animal might wash up on another con-tinent, too?

I guess it'll make it into the myth if it does.

The water is hot today. The long-eared animal bobs up and down in the water and moves its legs determinedly. The other day, I ground my husband's analogous bone into fine pieces and scattered them in the river. The sparkling grains floated on the water for a while before slipping under the surface.

That's a myth.

What's that? A myth?

I've never heard of anything like it. Have you?

The women giggle and continue murmuring to each other.

\ Narcissi \

I turned up today.

I opened the front door, and there stood a much younger me, with long hair.

"Well. I thought it had to be about time. It's good to see you," I said.

The me outside the door took a small step back.

"I remember that hairstyle," I said.

I seemed to be at a loss for what to say.

"So this is what I used to look like."

"It is. I know your face well. There's another you, about as old as you are, still alive back there," the me on the doorstep said quietly.

—

The two of us lived together from then on.

First of all, we decided how to split the housework. I liked cleaning, and had little interest in cooking. The other me felt the same, so rather than divide up the tasks, we decided to alternate according to the days of the week.

My cooking was plain fare.

"You're still young. Are you hungry for more meat, or fried foods?" I asked me, but I shook my head.

"I don't eat a lot of meat, or even fish . . . I like vegetables best."

"Is that right? It would seem that we're different in many small ways," I said.

My cleaning was a little more slapdash than mine. I took some time to show me how to use the broom and wring out a cloth.

"I only figured out how to do all this after I started living here, I guess," I said to myself.

I nodded. "That must be it. I enjoy cleaning, but I never had much opportunity for it back there."

My words suddenly reminded me of many things.

The place where I'd been raised was even farther to the north.

By the time I knew it, there were three of me. I was told that when we were born there had been ten, but seven had stunted.

"What does that mean, they stunted?" I asked the mothers, but they would only shake their heads.

"Things that live are things that die. In time."

Die. I didn't understand the meaning of the word until the cat I kept brought in a mouse. The mouse, which had always moved, stopped moving at all, and grew cold before my eyes.

There were many animals at that house. Cats. Dogs. Mice. Rabbits. Cows. Horses. Chickens. Bantams. Ducks. Geese. Peafowl. Dozens of waterbirds bobbed on the big lake in the garden. The one who liked to sit very still and watch the grebes dive was me, the shortest of us three.

"You like that? Just watching those birds go into the water?" I asked, and the shortest me nodded.

"Sometimes they dive for a long time, and sometimes they don't."

The mothers always told us how important it was to notice things. When the shortest me gave an account of the grebes over dinner, they were full of praise.

"Observe carefully. Never rush to conclusions. But commit everything to memory, without neglecting the smallest detail," they said.

We turned fifteen, and the shortest me quickly grew taller. Soon the three of us were all the same height, and not even the mothers were able to tell us apart.

We often fooled around and tried to trick the mothers.

There were several of them, and although each looked slightly different, overall they more or less resembled one another. Once, one of them left, and another came to take her place.

"I miss her," one of me said, but I didn't really understand what I meant.

The mothers were kind. But that was all. Like fishing floats spinning on the water, the mothers were always there, brightly hovering. They taught us how to cook and clean and launder, but when we tried to apply what we'd learned, they laughed and stopped us.

"You'll have more housework than you can shake a stick at soon enough," they said.

I'd never loved the mothers. Not until the great mother arrived.

The three of us slept in the same bed. We'd lie in a row, in no specific order.

The rhythms of our sleep were similar. When I woke, more often than not the other two would open their eyes, too.

We slept with the curtains open. The midnight moon shone through the window and cast its frame in shadow onto the floor.

I'd say, "Look, there," and the others would echo—*Look, there.*

The great mother arrived the day we turned seventeen.

"Happy birthday," the great mother said, and gave us a gift in a large cardboard box: a computer.

The great mother taught us how to use it. The three of

us were enchanted. We played games on it, and wrote, and designed pictures, and made music.

The great mother arrived and taught me the meaning of love.

"But you don't love one another?" the great mother asked.

I thought about it. There was a lot of time for thinking, so I thought about it for a very long time.

I loved me. But I also didn't love me.

Both these things were true, as far as I could tell.

The great mother I only loved.

I lived with the other two of me until we turned twenty-five. A few things happened in that time, but the most important for me was the great mother leaving.

"Well, this is goodbye," the great mother said on the day we turned twenty. That night she made our favorite dish: chicken pot pie.

She used butter churned from our cows' milk, eggs from our hens, a slaughtered cockerel, and wheat the mothers had harvested from the field.

"It tastes good."

The other two happily had the chicken pot pie, but my chest was full and I could eat only a little.

"Don't cry," the great mother said, as she wiped my tears with the palm of her hand. I hadn't realized I was crying.

That night I followed the great mother out of the house. I found her waiting for me beside the lake in the garden. Its shores were adorned by a tumult of white narcissi.

"Don't come after me."

"Why do you have to leave?"

"I realized I want to be somewhere else. Somewhere far away."

"Please don't."

"I'm going."

The great mother and I embraced. Her breasts were soft. I felt as if a lump of something was growing and filling me up somewhere under my navel. I sucked at her lips. She smelled good.

"Well," the great mother said, and looked distracted. "Your lips are like a spring snow."

I can no longer clearly recall the look that was on the great mother's face as she said this. It's far in the past now.

I didn't let her go for a long, long time. Even once the rooster had signaled dawn, we were still sitting on the grass, holding hands.

I was unable to get to my feet until the other two came and found me. I only vaguely remember how she looked when she left, but I remember her smell vividly. It was a beguiling scent, like narcissus.

I started my journey the autumn of the year I turned twenty-five.

Leaving the other two of me behind, I simply headed south.

It took a long voyage to get to this place. After setting out, I traveled through green fields for some time, but once I had crested the first mountains, there were hardly any plants to be seen.

I'd been given a compact hovercraft. It was powered by sunlight and wind, and inefficient. I dug for insects to eat when I could to make the food I'd brought with me go further.

Water, on the other hand, was abundant. Streams flowed everywhere through the barrens, and the sandbanks and shores harbored what few plants there were. When I was able to use the hovercraft to travel upstream, the going was easy. But the streams were too narrow and shallow more often than not.

I had no computer communication during my journey. Out in the wastelands there was no way to connect to what remained of the satellite network. I had to rely on a compass and the stars to track where I was. The mothers had taught me how to read the stars.

It took about three months to reach this place.

How relieved I was when the city came into view! I'd known for some time that I was getting close. There had been signs—small things indicating the presence of life. Hints that were neither sounds, nor smells, nor vibrations, and for which there were yet no words.

I'd imagined the city would have a castle wall, or a gate, but this one didn't.

"Sometimes you have a little trouble finding your way in," the mothers had said. But gradually the wastelands budded, shrubs and trees appeared, water became abundant, and the city glided serenely into view.

I hid the hovercraft in a ravine some distance away and made for my home, which I'd been told was in the north of the city.

How had I reacted then—the me that met me at the door?

I think I greeted me very calmly. I must have had a similar cast of mind, most likely, to how I was feeling now.

So many times I'd tried to picture the day when I would turn up. At first, of course, I'd resisted the idea. Once I turned forty the reluctance started to yield, bit by bit, and by the time I was fifty, it started to give my uneventful days a sense of purpose to turn my thoughts to how I might eventually appear before me.

"It's good to see you," I'd said to me that day, and welcomed me in.

For the next two months, we lived together.

The day I left, the skies foretold snow. Goodbye, I waved, and started walking toward the ravine where I had hidden the hovercraft.

As I watched me walk away, I recalled the day the great mother had left. It had been a balmy spring day. The warmth of the great mother's body as we sat next to each other on the grass. Once night fell, though, the air had cooled. We had pressed our shoulders close, and clasped our hands in each other's. When tears rolled down my cheeks, the great mother had dried them with her handkerchief.

The great mother had kept turning around to look behind her. When dawn broke and she slowly started walking, prompted by the two who found me and the other mothers, she looked back toward us repeatedly, as though searching for something in my expression. But unlike her, the me who left that day when the clouds were heavy with snow walked away without turning back at all. Resolutely, toward the ravine.

What had I been thinking of as I walked away? And how much had I, left alone in this house until the next me arrived, thought of it since?

"I never knew there would be so many people here," said the me with the long hair. I sounded happy. I reminded me of myself when I had first arrived.

It was true that unlike back there where we were raised, this city contained many men and many women, with faces unlike ours, different bodies. And children.

"It's strange to think there are humans who aren't me."

"The mothers weren't us," I said.

The me with the long hair looked doubtful. "But the mothers are creations."

"So are we."

"No—unlike them, we're alive."

"The mothers also live."

"Depending on how you define life, perhaps."

I had no time left. Now that the new me was here, I would have to leave in two months, like the me before me had done.

"Do you think you've gotten the hang of operating the carousel?"

"It's simple enough."

My ostensible position here was as the carousel attendant at the park.

"The park is a good place for keeping watch," said the me with the long hair, and smiled.

"Observe carefully. Never rush to conclusions. But commit everything to memory, without neglecting the smallest detail." I repeated the words the mothers had taught me long ago.

The me with the long hair nodded gravely. "I will: Observe carefully. Never rush to conclusions. But commit everything to memory, without neglecting the smallest detail. The mothers used to tell me that, too."

The word *mothers* felt like a thorn to my heart. Although I had lived in this city for a long time now, I had thought about the great mother often. Though her face had long since been worn down to a pale dim blur of a memory, I had continued to think of her, again and again.

"In the spring, the garden comes up in white narcissus," I said to the long-haired me.

"Did you say narcissus?"

"Narcissus, as well as viola, crocus, tulips, anemones, wild strawberries."

"You've planted so many different kinds."

"Each of us did, over the years."

"I love flowers, too. Spring flowers especially."

"The narcissus was mine."

Soon I would be leaving behind the me with the long hair to be the new carousel attendant.

The night before the day I was due to leave, the me with the long hair held a party for me. It was just the two of us, with chicken pot pie, sautéed spinach, and champagne.

"I was never this good of a cook," I said, and the me with the long hair smiled.

"I didn't realize we'd be different in so many small ways."

"How could we not be? We start with the same genes, but our environment and the many accidents of chance make each of us slightly different."

The me with the long hair looked downward for a while. Then I raised my head and looked at me. "I wonder if I'll make a good watcher."

"You will. Remember, the whole reason we were given this work was that we are naturally suited to it."

"Of course. You're right."

The wine was good. As was the chicken pot pie. I didn't usually eat such rich food, but it must have been skillfully prepared, because it wasn't heavy at all.

The night got late, and the sounds of the city had quieted down.

"This is my favorite time of day."

"Why is that?"

"I can feel all the people out there fast asleep."

It was the same hint of life I had sensed when I first approached this city. Strangely, I felt it most strongly not during the day, when the humans were awake, but late at night, when the city was hushed and sleeping.

The me with the long hair looked at me again, as if to say something, before seeming to decide not to. After a while, I asked quietly: "Why is it that we don't have names?"

The question had never occurred to me. "There's no rule against it."

"Have you never wanted to give yourself a name?"

"No, never."

"Why?"

"Who would there be to call me by it?"

Having said so, I suddenly felt lonely. But it was only for a moment. The loneliness passed swiftly.

"I will. For the few hours we still have together."

"There's no need."

"Even so."

This long-haired me was more sentimental, I thought. "What would you call yourself, then, if you could have a name?"

"Well, I thought perhaps I could be Pater."

"Pater." It had a strange sound. It felt unfamiliar, but it was easy to say. "Does it mean anything?"

"I don't know, but it forms a pair with Mother—or so I'm told."

I wasn't sure what I meant, but the plosive sound was pleasing. I repeated the word several times under my breath— *Pater, Pater.*

–

The following day augured snow, just like the day the old me had left.

"Goodbye, then," I said, and turned away from myself.

"Wait," I heard me say behind me.

I turned around.

"Would you—would you say my name again, when you go?"

"Okay."

"Thank you."

"Goodbye, Pater."

"Goodbye."

We waved at each other. Then, without turning around again, I went toward the riverbank where the me with the long hair said I had hidden the hovercraft.

I left the city. The greenery became sparse and then desolate. Snow was beginning to lie on the ground. *Pater*, I said to myself. I felt a faint desire to see the great mother. Had my predecessors planted the viola and crocus and tulips and anemones and wild strawberries so they might recall similar memories? I wanted to listen to her tell me about them. I felt certain it was something we could have shared.

Many more of me would yet be born, but I didn't have much longer to live. *Goodbye*, I repeated silently to the many of me I'd never meet, then carefully brushed away the dusting of snow that had started to settle on my garment.

/ *Green Garden* /

A long time ago, my mother told me the meaning of my name, Rien.

"In summer, at daybreak, the flower with your name makes a sound as it blooms."

I first saw that flower around the time my breasts were budding. My garment rubbed my nipples and made them sore. Let's make you a garment out of softer cloth, my mother said gently.

The flowers with my name opened one after another on the surface of the lake at the far end of the garden. I liked the white blooms best. It was rare that I heard it, but a few times, at least, I caught the sound of their opening. It sounded like a sigh.

By the time I'd worn out the garment my mother had sewn
me from soft cloth, my nipples had stopped being painful.

We'll need to think about a man, my mother started to say.

A man. The sound of the word was strange to me. At that
time, I had yet to see a man, but my mother had told me
about them often.

"Are they like you, or me, or Hawa, or are they an entirely
different thing?"

"Oh, men aren't things. They're people, like us."

Then why had we never seen one?

"Men are very busy."

Busy. It was still some time before I'd know the meaning
of the word.

Hawa and I strolled around the garden every day.

Hawa was the same age as me.

The population density was extremely low where we
lived. So for a long time after I was born, the only people I
knew were my mother and Hawa, and Hawa's mother.

It was a half-hour walk through the garden to get to
Hawa's house.

By the time I finished doing laundry and cleaning and
studying, it would be around three in the afternoon. On
Mondays, Wednesdays, and Fridays, I visited Hawa. Tuesdays, Thursdays, and Saturdays, Hawa came to me. We
walked around the garden and tended to the plants, chased
insects, and played until the sun went down.

After supper, when we'd finished our homework, the

mother of the one who was visiting would come over, through the dark, with a lantern in her hand.

Insects always flocked to the lantern. We'd wave good-bye, and the one left behind would stay there standing in the darkness for a while.

The night was long, and by the time I'd taken a bath and was listening to the stories my mother told me, I'd start to get sleepy. But if I let myself fall asleep then, I often ended up wide awake in the middle of the night, so I tried to fight it.

Soon, though, my eyelids would get heavy, and my mother would tell me to go to bed. I slipped into sleep to the sound of rain and insects' wings.

The man's brows were thick, just like his arms.

His hair was mixed with gray and his cheeks were creased. So this was a man. I looked hard at him.

I had known for a month that a man would be arriving. Hawa and I had both just turned eighteen. The man was expressionless. But perhaps they were born that way. How should I know? I found him frightening.

"I'll be staying here for some time," the man said, entrusting himself to the recliner. I thought he looked tired.

"How would you like your dinner?" my mother asked.

The man looked at me closely, as though in return for earlier.

He said, "I think I'll eat with you. I guess this young lady's never met a man before. See? She's scared."

I thought I was hiding it, but he'd seen straight through me. My cheeks flushed hot.

"That's a good look on you," he said, and lifted the ends of his mouth just slightly.

After the man came, my mother's cooking changed.

"A good cook. I'm in luck," the man said, but the rich, dripping cuts of beef and lamb weren't much to my taste.

"Don't you want that?"

He skewered the meat I'd left uneaten with his fork, and put it on his own plate. I stared at him, and he shrugged.

"Don't you know about all the places that don't get enough to eat?"

I didn't answer him. My mother didn't tell me a lot about that kind of thing. I mainly learned about the way the human body worked, and how to grow plants, and how to move to keep myself safe.

The man made himself at home in the room at the end of the hallway.

"How long will he stay?" I asked my mother in private.

She shook her head.

"That's not for us to decide. In time, what will happen will happen, and things will happen as they will."

I had no idea what she meant. There were many things I didn't know in this world, but those were things like when the rain would come or the wind would start up, or how the water would shift, or when the insects would swarm. I'd simply never dreamed that a person—like me and my mother and Hawa—could be the cause of so much uncertainty.

—

It happened in the night.

I sensed the man was near me.

I heard his voice say, "Would you prefer some light?" and the door opened quietly.

I couldn't speak. My body froze and my skin broke out in goose bumps.

The man stood by my bed.

"Can I come in?"

I still couldn't move. My mother had taught me how my body had the ability to take in a man's sperm, and how one of my eggs could be infiltrated by the man's sperm and start dividing, just as a plant was pollinated and made seed. But whether the ordeal would befall me that night, not for a long time yet, or thankfully never—that was far beyond my ken.

That's for the man to decide, my mother had said.

Why? Why can't it be for me to decide? I asked, affronted.

In the far past, there were times that women decided, and times that women and men decided together by talking, and times when it didn't need thinking about at all—or so they say. Of course, at that time, there was an equal number of women and men, not like we have now, when there are fewer than twenty for all so many of us.

Why are there more women than men? It isn't like that with plants. Plants usually have both male and female organs, and even when the sexes are separated, the numbers are roughly the same.

It's because women are stronger.

Women were stronger, so my mother had told me, but the man's strength was far greater than mine. I was filled with humiliation and pain, and just a hint of satisfaction. I couldn't enjoy what he did, but he had a pleasant smell. It reminded me of the way the garden smelled when the green was at its thickest.

I became pregnant.

The man stayed around while the fetus grew, although I didn't see him every day.

"Men are busy," my mother said, like I'd heard her say before.

Days I smelled meat grilling were days when the man would stay the night. I started being able to tell by what my mother cooked for supper.

The months passed, and the baby was a girl.

"Look, her face is different from yours. Aren't genes wonderful?" my mother said dreamily.

I'd rarely seen Hawa since the man arrived. When my child was half a year old, I walked through the garden and went to visit her for the first time in a while.

I cut an armful of eucalyptus shoots on my way. Hawa was partial to their smell.

When I got near her house, I heard a sound like a kitten coming through the branches.

"Hello," I said from the porch, and Hawa's mother came bustling out.

"Oh, Rien, how have you been?" Hawa's mother asked, looking happy.

"Where's Hawa?" I asked.

With a smile on her face, she said, "Hawa just gave birth yesterday."

Hawa's baby was also a girl, who looked a lot like mine.

"Of course, half of your and Hawa's genes came from the same man to begin with," my mother said.

I'd known since I was a child that my father and Hawa's father were the same man, but I didn't understand what that meant until I had my own child.

The children were very alike, but Hawa's child's eyes were a pale brown, and my child's were a blue that was closer to gray.

When the children were nearly two years old, I got pregnant again. So did Hawa.

The months passed, and we each had another girl.

The man had left my house. But he often called when the moon in the sky was at its quarter, and shared my bed.

I had four children who shared the man's genes, and Hawa had five. The children were all girls. The mothers came to give us a helping hand. I hadn't seen the mothers in years. They weren't posted here permanently, because my mother had only one child, but they had sometimes stayed with us for a time after a big storm or a flood.

I liked having children, both birthing them and raising them. My days were busy, and the mothers attentive.

In time, my mother and Hawa's mother retreated to the end of the garden.

"Be well," my mother said to me kindly.

My chest felt full, and I couldn't seem to look her in the eye.

"Don't worry. You can come visit anytime."

As we watched our mothers leave, Hawa looked thoughtful.

"Have you ever wondered about our mothers' mothers? Where do you think they are?"

I had wondered about that, too, from time to time, ever since I'd had my first child.

"Those humans have already aged and died," the mothers told us.

"Where do humans go when they die?"

"They are laid to rest in the garden. There they are broken down and eventually returned to the world."

My mother had taught me the same thing. But in the same way as I hadn't known how I could be made fertile until the first time I lay with the man, I couldn't imagine yet what it was to be broken down and returned to the world.

The man died.

We held a funeral. The four mothers, Hawa and I, and our nine children carried the man's body to the end of the garden and laid him on the green brush.

The man looked far more beautiful than he had when he was alive.

"Why does dying make you go pale?" Hawa's third daughter asked.

"Why indeed?" the mothers wondered. "We don't often see bodies, so we don't know either."

It was the season for rain. The greenery gave off a thick smell, and it seemed like the perfect day for his funeral.

"What happens if we leave him here?" Hawa's youngest child asked.

"He will be taken apart by animals and insects and broken down by microorganisms until only his bones are left, and they, too, will return to the soil in time."

"I feel sorry for him."

"There's no need for that. It's a very good thing."

I'd seen much less of the man lately, so I was surprised when he chose to die at my house.

"I loved you, you know," the man had said to me, just before he died.

I wasn't sure what to say, and only nodded vaguely.

"Well, is that all? So many of the others were smitten with me."

I nodded a little again. I didn't mind him, but I knew that was different from love. I smiled at him to keep the peace, like the mothers often did.

"That's more like it. I always liked seeing you smile. Not that you ever smiled much for me."

Within a few months, the man was broken down completely. Hawa's youngest had been going to see him every week.

"You said it's a good thing, didn't you?" the child said, suspiciously.

"Yes, a very good thing," the mothers all agreed.

The children grew quickly. I taught them many things, as my mother had taught me. But on top of that, the mothers were teaching them other things that I'd never learned.

"You were an only child, but there are four of them. That has brought a new social structure into being, small though it may be."

When the number of humans reached a certain threshold, that created a society, the mothers said, but I didn't really know what that meant. Well, I knew what it meant—just not what it was.

"The purpose of study is to learn things you have not experienced," the mothers said.

My first daughter turned eighteen. They said a man would be coming soon.

I thought this meant I would have another child, but I was wrong. My daughter would be the one having a child, and this man and I would never share a bed.

"It would complicate the determination of future inbreeding risks," the mothers explained.

I began living as through a fog. I started visiting Hawa again on Mondays, Wednesdays, and Fridays, and on Tuesdays, Thursdays, and Saturdays, she came to me. But the time I spent with Hawa was no longer carefree like it had been before.

"I wonder what this man will be like," I said.

Hawa shrugged. "It makes no difference to me. I don't want to have any more children. You don't either, do you, Rien?"

I didn't know.

The man was called Kuan.

"The man before never had a name," I said, looking at him. Kuan smiled.

"I had a brother. So we were given names to tell us apart."
The mothers nodded. Of course. The bloodline was known for producing boys. Lovely. How wonderful.
"Why is it wonderful when a boy is born?"
Because there are so few of them. They're fragile. And rare. The mothers talked over one another in low voices like ripples on the water.
My first child became pregnant straightaway and had a girl. Hawa's first daughter also had a girl.
Kuan didn't stay in my house. But he didn't stay with Hawa, either.
"I prefer to sleep out in the green."
He pitched a tent in the garden and lived there, and cooked for himself, too. The mothers seemed displeased, but Kuan took no notice. Every day, I watched the smoke of his cook fire rise over the tops of the trees.

Kuan was just the same age as me.
I asked him about the women he had visited before coming here. How they would speak. How they spent their day. How they handled plants. How they raised children. What they were like when they coupled.
Kuan told me everything easily. I listened to his words like I was listening to stories of faraway lands.
"The man who was here before you loved me. But I didn't feel any way about him."
"That's too bad."
"Are there any women you've loved, Kuan?"

Kuan was silent for some time.

"I've never thought about it. Like and love—those are feelings I've had only for the mother that raised me, and for my brothers."

I was a little surprised. I'd never had any kind of feeling toward the mothers. They had always just been there when they were needed. Unchanging.

"Some mothers leave."

"Why?"

"They reach the end of their life."

"They die?"

"Not quite the same as dying, I think. But not too different."

"Then they get returned afterward?"

"Again, not quite. But you could think of it that way, broadly speaking."

I felt frightened. I looked up at Kuan. The trees were a deep green, and maybe that was why his face looked so pale. I suddenly wanted to have a child. I said so to him. He pulled me into his tent.

For the first time, I cried out as we coupled.

When they found out I was pregnant, the mothers shut me in the room at the back of the house. There was no window, but there were three locks on the door.

When the months had passed, a baby boy was born to me.

The mothers came and took him. I screamed and cried, but the mothers locked the door again.

After a long time, they finally let me out of the room. My first daughter had had another girl and was pregnant with her third child. I searched all through the house, but the boy I'd birthed was nowhere to be found. Kuan's tent was gone, too.

"Where's Kuan?"

"He left. But the next man's here, so it's okay," my first daughter said, and smiled at me. "You were gone for quite a while. The mothers said you went on a trip. Did you like it?"

The next man was a fat man. He had a shiny face and was always sweating. *Where's Kuan*, I asked the mothers, but they only kept moving around sedately, murmuring, *Don't know, don't know.*

Each day, I thought about Kuan, and about the boy they had taken away.

I asked the next man to couple with me, but he refused. "Haven't you had enough children?" he said pityingly.

"There's nothing but green out here," Hawa says, looking up at the treetops.

Hawa is the only one who still comes to visit me at the end of the garden.

The birds are crying.

ck ck ck ck ck

pop pop pop pop

trrrrrrrrr

long long long

The plumeria and bougainvillea grow so lushly it's as if

they're advancing toward us. White and yellow and violet orchids court insects fiercely, and longan fruits keep falling.

"The garden is always so wild," Hawa murmurs. There are wrinkles around her mouth and across her brow where they weren't when she was young.

"Do you remember the first man?" I ask Hawa. I trace her wrinkles with my finger.

"I do. But not too clearly anymore."

Hawa touches my face, gently. Then we walk to the lake and listen to the sound of lotus flowers opening. Day is about to break.

"I can't seem to sleep much recently. I suppose I'll die before very long."

"Then we can both return here together."

Remember how my youngest kept going to see his body? Hawa says. *She said the bones were a brilliant white. She said she's never seen such a beautiful white.*

"Hawa—were you ever in love?"

Hawa thinks for a while. Then, in a voice like a whisper, she says, "Never."

Another lotus blossom opens with a sound like a sigh.

| The Dancing Child |

The child was trouble from the start.

Each time the child did something unforeseen, it sent the mothers to their wits' end. "It's been several hundred years since we saw a child like this," one mother sighed.

"You're right. The records say another child like this was born once before," said another.

Yes, in which case, we should be able to find out what to do, shouldn't we? the mothers said among themselves.

"Yes, but this child is different from that one."

That's true, you're right, they said again and again, speaking over one another. The mothers' clothes rustled smoothly. All the mothers were dressed in many layers of fine white cloth.

The child was very active. From sunup to sundown, it rooted in every corner, pulled up every plant, picked up and sniffed every tiny creature, and sometimes put them in its mouth and ate them.

On the child's second birthday, it swallowed the fruit of a poison tree and nearly died. The child had suddenly broken out in a cold sweat and started stumbling and writhing about in agony. Not knowing the cause, the mothers descended into panic. Finally, one of them recalled that the child had been playing under the tree that morning, and quickly compounded the antidote.

The child was unlike any the mothers had raised before.

"The other children were all cautious."

"Yes, and each one was quiet."

"They warmed to you, if you showed them affection."

"And they always did exactly what you told them to."

The mothers spoke among themselves discreetly. None of the other children had questioned what the mothers said, or tried to probe into what they were thinking. They had followed the mothers' guidance obediently, grown swiftly, and then, once grown, had become watchers. But this child sniffed around the mothers, doubted them, tried to outdo them, and, given the slightest opening, delighted in outwitting them.

For the first time in a long time, the mothers started to put safeguards in place.

The children who were destined to become watchers were made a few at a time, from a handful of lineages.

Each sector grew children from only one lineage. This meant all of the watchers growing in that sector were genetically identical.

"But every child has their quirks," the mothers said.

"Just because this one is terribly individual, it isn't necessarily cause for concern," they told one another. But the mothers kept a careful eye on the child.

The child grew steadily. It turned three, then five, then ten. The mothers created a few extra children, just in case. They decided to keep the child in a house with six of its siblings, thinking their equanimity and obedience might rub off. But the child didn't change one whit.

Lineages suited to watching—that was what the mothers were supposed to be growing, needed to be growing. To watch tirelessly, but never take action by themselves; to observe, and record, and report. These genetics had always resulted in humans that felt satisfaction and pride at dedicating their lives to this duty. But the child refused to observe anything.

"I'd rather be the one being watched than watch," the child said.

The child especially liked to strip off the white cloths that the mothers wore, sew them into oddly shaped costumes, and dance around in the woods.

"Why don't you all want to dance with me? It's real fun," the child asked, but the other children looked confused.

I don't know how.

What's dancing good for, anyway?

But the child's enthusiasm wasn't dampened. The child sewed up a whole stack of costumes and handed them out to the other children. A couple of them joined the child in the woods and tried dancing.

"Can we allow this?" the mothers worried.

The mothers met many times to discuss the issue. Eventually, they decided to send the child to the great mother who lived by the river. The great mother had arrived in this sector just recently.

"It'll be the two of us from now on," the great mother said, crouching down until she was eye to eye with the child, who laughed loudly.

"You look even more strange than the mothers!"

The great mother sighed, then stood up swiftly. From her full height, she said, "Get changed and get ready for your lessons."

The child's questions always caught the great mother off guard.

What's outside this sector?

When can I leave the sector and see what's outside?

The child pestered the great mother incessantly, with questions about trees and the stars in the night sky, what was up the river, dreams, nightmares, the mothers, the other children the child had been with before, and everything that could conceivably come to pass.

"Why do you find everything so interesting as you do?" the great mother retorted.

Surprised, the child asked yet another question. "Doesn't everybody?"

The great mother shrugged and said, "Not your siblings, at least."

The great mother took pains to give the child answers that were as full and accurate as she could. About the weather and geography; ecosystems, planetary and other celestial bodies, the animal kingdom; about life, how it worked and how it came to be.

"Are you alive, Great Mother?" the child asked, innocently.

"Of course I am. Though in a different way than you."

"Huh," the child said, and dropped the subject, for once.

The child turned eleven, then twelve, then thirteen. The great mother gave them a wide-ranging education. The child's frequent questions kept interrupting, but she was able to take them and incorporate them into the learning. The child seemed to be coming along well and becoming less capricious over the years. It was only the dancing that the child refused to stop.

The great mother had settled by the bank of a large river. Past early summer, the weather turned wild, and the river rose and turned the color of mud. The child loved to watch the water after a storm.

"Look at it go," the child would say, enraptured.

The great mother warned that the child must never go into the river after a storm. A few times, the child had gone up the river in a small craft, but always accompanied by the great mother. The child had rowed a craft alone a few times, but only within the great mother's sight.

"One of these days, I'm going to row all the way to the end of the river," the child told the great mother.

"That's dangerous."

"I don't care, I'll be much bigger and stronger by then."

"You think you know it all."

The child was indignant. Of course I don't. Because you never let me have any freedom. How can I possibly learn anything about the world when I'm stuck in the same tiny place?

The great mother sighed. Why do you always have to be like this?

"I can't help it. Don't look like that. Are you sad? Great Mother, you're my favorite. I'm not trying to leave you. I just want to know what else is out there."

The mothers and the great mother discussed the question of when the child would be ready for a computer.

Some of the mothers said, "What's the worst that could happen? The child is so young." But others shook their heads.

"We've gone to such lengths to isolate the child with the great mother—perhaps a computer is a bad idea. That child is a little dangerous. What's known can't be forgotten, but what's never been seen can't be imagined."

"But then the child will never be a watcher. Without a computer, how would we even maintain a line of communication?"

The great mother weighed the mothers' opinions carefully.

In the end, the child was given a computer on its seventeenth birthday, the same as the other children.

At first, the child didn't seem particularly impressed with the computer, but after a while, the child learned to use it

exactly as it liked. Although the computer wasn't connected
to a network, every computer issued to the children came
with a copy of all human common knowledge stored on its
internal memory. Soon the child became enamored with it.

"This should tell you everything you could ever want to
know," the great mother said kindly, and patted the child's
head.

The computer's great, but my birthday cake was wonderful, the child said, shyly. You're the best, Great Mother.
Thanks for everything.

This wasn't the first time a child she was raising had
said something like this, but the great mother stopped and
thought.

Why, I feel about this child the same as this child feels
about me. That's never happened before.

The great mother tried to express that the child was special to her, too, but she couldn't seem to find the words. Instead, she said, "I think the computer will be very useful to
you. Study hard and try to make the most of what you've
been given."

The child kept dancing.

The child liked dancing on the riverbank best. One
day, the dancing child stepped into the forest. Somewhere in
the forest, there should have been several houses where the
other children lived, but the child hadn't seen any of them
for a few years now.

The forest was more humid than the child remembered,

and full of a vegetal scent. The trees grew close to one another and their canopies cut off the sunlight. The child went on deep and deeper, still dancing, and reached a place where the light shone in.

"Oh!" the child gasped, quietly.

A girl carrying a basket on her back was picking plants.

"What are you . . . doing?" the child asked the girl.

"Gathering herbs," the girl said.

The child and the girl stared at each other.

"You look the same as me," the child said.

"Of course. We're siblings, aren't we?" the girl said.

A faint memory came back to the child: of being young and sleeping in the same bed with several others. Looking at the same things and laughing at the same things at the same time. Playing and pretending. And dancing together.

"What are you doing?" the girl asked.

"Dancing," said the child.

From that day, the child and the girl started to meet from time to time in the spot where the sunlight shone.

One day, the girl brought a strangely formed child's garment with her. It was a dancing costume the child had once sewn.

"Do you remember this?"

"I remember!" the child shouted, snatching the garment from her hand.

"Oh!" The girl was startled. None of her siblings ever moved so roughly.

"What's wrong?" the child asked.

The girl showed the child the back of her hand. It was bleeding.

"I'm sorry," the child said, and took the girl's hand and licked it. The girl giggled. The child felt a strange hard lump make its way around their body. Blood coursed through them like the flow of the great river in the middle of a storm.

"Let's dance," the child suggested.

The girl took a step, hesitantly. She copied the child's movements as best she could. The child wrapped the white garment around their shoulders, and when they started to sweat, they passed the garment to the girl, who took it and wrapped it around her neck. They danced until sunset.

The child was about to turn twenty-five.

"You'll soon become a watcher and start your journey," the great mother said. The child—who was no longer a child, but would always be hers—looked thoughtful.

"How many years will it be before I can come back?"

"That would have been covered in your learning," the great mother said, although she knew full well that wasn't what the child was asking.

"I don't want to go. I'm staying with you."

The child ran outside and went to the place in the forest where the sun shone, and danced to their heart's content. It had been a while since the child had seen the girl there. The child surmised that she must have been forbidden from coming. The child was right. The child had enjoyed dancing with her, but there was nothing wrong with dancing alone, either.

The child was happy as long as they could be near the great mother.

The great mother approached quietly, pushing the plants aside.

"Even if you stay, I can't live with you anymore," the great mother said. She watched the child dance for a while.

The child went on dancing without saying a word.

"How beautifully you dance," the great mother said.

The child ran to the great mother. They cried great tears. The great mother didn't cry, because she couldn't. Instead, she stroked the child's head, on and on.

The rumor went around the mothers that the great mother might be near death.

"This great mother appeared about a hundred and fifty years ago, didn't she?"

"It could be time soon."

The great mother had stopped showing up to the mothers' gatherings. She retreated to her home and sat at her computer all day long, waiting to hear from the child. The child rarely wrote, so she looked through her albums of pictures she had of the child, and reread the child's old essays, and went through the results of the child's biannual physical scans.

"At least they're keeping well," the great mother said to herself.

Every watcher was replaced with a new generation as soon as the scan found any abnormalities or signs of aging.

The great mother withdrew from helping raise the children in the area.

"Let's leave her in peace," the mothers said to one another.

Meanwhile, the child had traveled down the great river by hovercraft, arrived at their watching post, and settled in. It was a region rich in vegetation, where people lived in houses with gardens. The gardens were strange to the child. In the place they'd grown up, all the plants had been wild and free.

The child found and visited the old watcher.

"Hello."

"Welcome," the watcher said, and smiled. "Did you have a hard journey?"

"Nope, not at all. It was an adventure."

The watcher looked at the child curiously. "You're very different from me. We look the same, but—how can I say it?—you remind me of the women around here. No—that's not exactly it. You're more like the men." The old watcher laughed. "Why, it's been a while since anything made me laugh aloud," she said, and put her arms around the child's shoulders.

How frail her body is compared to the great mother, the child thought. I miss her. So the child danced a little.

The watcher laughed again.

She's laughing, but she still looks sad, the child thought.

The child spent two months with the previous watcher, as was the rule. After that, the old watcher would depart, and the child would become the new watcher. The child had been told by the great mother that this region had an extremely low number of breeding men and would require special care to watch over.

The women generally had several children each. The mothers who were sent to raise the children seemed a little different from the mothers of the sector where the child had come from. They looked the same, but felt emptier than the mothers who had raised the child, or the great mother.

The women didn't live very long. After they had birthed a few babies, they aged quickly and retired to tents in the corners of their gardens, or formed communes among themselves, and lived quietly.

The child was more interested in the men than the women. There were only a few of them, but each one was very individual.

One day, the child met a woman called Rien. Watchers weren't forbidden to socialize with those of the region, but they were supposed to refrain from relating to them in a way that would interfere with their lives.

Interfere? It's not as if I could have any influence on the women and men here, just by myself, the child thought.

The child's impressions of the region were very different from what they had expected from learning about it with the great mother.

Rien enjoyed the child's dancing. It had become the child's habit to dance daily. The child's post in the region was supposed to be as gardener, so the child took care of the gardens every day. That said, the local mothers usually kept the gardens in shape, so there wasn't much for the child to do.

When Rien saw the child dancing, she said, "How beautifully you dance," just like the great mother used to say.

The child was glad and kept on dancing. Rien watched them without getting bored. Soon, though, the child started to feel very sad. The child thought they knew something about this sadness. It had the same nature as the sadness they had noticed in the old watcher.

(But my sadness is a little different from the old watcher's, it seems.)

The child went on dancing until they collapsed in exhaustion. Rien watched them the entire time.

After some time, Rien died. The child went and watched over her bones every day until they scattered to the winds. The child had noticed that there was one man who sometimes came to visit Rien's bones.

"Hi, who are you?" the child asked.

The man shook his head, but after a while, he pointed to the bones and said, "Do you know her?"

The child nodded.

"She was my mother. I never got to live with her. But I loved her."

The child knew the meaning of the word *love*, but this was the first time they had heard a human use it.

"What does it mean, to love someone?" the child asked.

"It means you want to be with them," the man said.

The child started dancing. The man watched them intently. The child didn't get sad. Not in the way they'd always

felt sad when Rien had watched them. The child danced for
a while and then went back to gardening. They thought they
would like to see the great mother. Late that night, the child
opened the computer and sent a message. The great mother's
replies had been lagging recently.

When the message arrived that the great mother had died,
the child took to bed. The mothers of the region took turns
looking after them. The child didn't recover for almost half
a year. One night, a man visited them. It was the man who
had visited Rien's bones. The man looked down at the child.

"You lost someone you loved," the man said.

The child nodded.

"Do you want to have sex?" he asked.

The child felt torn, but then said yes.

He did it respectfully and thoroughly. The child liked it.

Is this interfering? the child wondered for a moment,
before realizing they didn't care. There was something hot
rising inside them that they recalled they had once been full
of. What have I been doing all this time? the child wondered.
But being a watcher was the only life they knew. The child
sensed within themself something of the bursting curiosity
toward the world they'd had before.

When they finished, the man said, "That's the only way I
know of making a woman feel better."

The child laughed. I do feel better. Thank you.

The mothers discovered the child's pregnancy at their
next scan, six months later.

–

The child had a baby boy.

The mothers swiftly took the baby away and called in the next watcher. The child settled among the women of the region and went on to have several more children: three girls and five boys, including the first. The child named the first girl Rien.

The mothers debated the wisdom of continuing to use the child's lineage to create further watchers, but because no more children were born with the child's unusual personality, the line escaped termination. It is not known whether the child's sons and daughters had issue themselves, or what influence they had on the world. And, finally, after a long intervening period, the great mother who died was reborn— but that is a story to be told at another time.

| Under the Eye of the Big Bird |

When I got on the fossil-fuel school bus, Jaden was sitting in my seat.

"Move," I said, but Jaden ignored me, of course. The bus started to move and I almost had to put a hand on his knee. I braced my legs and saved myself.

Inside my backpack, my lunch clattered. Mom slept in today, so she put two things wrapped in paper in my lunch box. Probably a big bag of crackers and a whole wheel of cheese. Go ahead and eat the whole thing if you want, Mom had said agreeably, and yawned wide.

I sat in the back seat and looked out the window. Mr. O'Neal passed us in the bicycle lane. There was a birdcage in his front basket. Inside, a brightly colored bird. Abigail once told me the bird was a hornbill.

I thought I'd see Abigail in class today, but she wasn't there.

The teacher gave us the assignment and then immediately turned to the desk and opened their notebook. We all opened our notebooks, too. I was really happy when I got to fourth grade and got more books. I love reading.

We have a lot of books at home. Dad reads them. He says I mustn't tell my friends how many books we have. Why, I ask him, and he laughs and says, Because. He still thinks of me as a kid. He probably doesn't even realize that I've been reading his books.

What happened to Abigail? Maybe she has a cold. She often spends time in the fifth- and sixth-grade classrooms, skipping grades, but on Wednesdays she's usually in class with us, in her real grade.

Abigail and I have been best friends ever since kindergarten. I know all her secrets, and she knows mine. When she went out with a sixth grader the other week, he kissed her. Did it taste sweet, I asked, and she smiled knowingly and said, Yeah, like cinnamon candy. The line of three gold earrings on her ear sparkled.

When Abigail wasn't around, I always ate lunch alone. On the bench under the row of poplars in the playground when it was sunny, and under the piano in the music room when it rained.

I never have much of an appetite. Partly because Mom's lunches are never that appetizing, but also because I'm just not that interested in food. I don't much like seeing other people eat, either. Aside from Abigail, I mean.

Abigail eats in a way that makes everything look good. Whether she's biting into a normal apple, or eating a regular old ham, cheese, and tomato sandwich, in Abigail's mouth, everything looks like a holiday feast. When I toy with the half of a bread roll I can't finish, Abigail reaches for it and takes it from me, and tears small pieces off it and brings them to her mouth. Tempted, I reach out, too. Abigail puts the rest of the roll back onto my palm and looks at me and smiles. When all of it is safely in my belly, Abigail pokes my cheek with her finger, and says, "Good girl, good girl."

Quit making fun of me, I say, but she doesn't stop smiling.

It was raining, and Abigail wasn't there, so I crawled under the piano and took the big bag of crackers and the wheel of cheese out of my lunch box and lined them up on a napkin.

Obviously, I didn't feel like eating either.

With a sigh, I put both of them back into my lunch box and closed its lid. I crawled out from under the piano and opened a window in the music room. I could smell the rain. Beyond the playground fence, Mr. O'Neal rode by on his bicycle. As usual, his front basket had the hornbill in its cage. In the rain, he looked like something other than human.

That afternoon, my luck ran out—Jaden decided to pick on me during free discussion.

Free discussion was already my least favorite class. You choose a topic and present your "truly free" opinion, and if someone disagrees, then you argue about it.

First off, I didn't like the whole idea of having to pick a topic. People always suggested dumb ones such as What pet would you like to have, or What should be in the town museum, or When and who would you marry. I could never come up with a "truly free" opinion about any of these.

Once, I suggested Where would you go if you were to leave this town and go live somewhere else, but the teacher shot it down. Why, Emma, would you suggest something as irrelevant as that? the teacher said, sounding extremely unimpressed, and wrinkled her nose. I heard Jaden tittering. The teacher turned to him immediately and said, Jaden, if you have the time to laugh at a classmate, maybe you can share your idea for a topic with the class. Jaden turned scarlet and looked down at his knees. I tried to make myself small, too. It was right for the teacher to be fair, but I didn't want anything to set Jaden off.

Why did Jaden always have to pick on me? Abigail said, I think he likes you, but I was sure that wasn't it. He hated me. And I preferred not to think about why.

Free might be the most-used word at our school.

Free thinking is more important than anything else, the teacher would say, at least three times a day.

But I never felt too free at school. Of course, the teachers never said anything to us even if we acted out a little. We were supposed to ask any questions we had in class. We could also ask to have a conversation with the principal. As long as you showed up to class, they didn't make you do anything, or tell us what we couldn't do, and we weren't supposed to get in trouble for bringing drugs or guns to school.

But, in fact, none of us makes a habit of pursuing questions during class, no one wants to have a conversation with the principal if they can help it, and guns are practically nonexistent in this town anyway—aside from the impressive collection of hunting rifles the eccentric Andersons are supposed to have in a shed at their property just outside the town limits—and no one bothers with drugs after the first couple of times, because the brief trip isn't worth getting found out and being forced to take the antitoxin. The hangover from the antitoxin they keep in the infirmary is pretty terrible.

Sure, we're free. The more we come up with ideas that aren't beholden to common sense, the more the teachers like it. Take a leap, they always say. Think outside the box. Sometimes, though, I ask Abigail, Do you think we really have to?

Don't worry, it's easy, Abigail says. Hop, step, fly. That's all it takes. You don't need to go far. You just need to be one step ahead of everyone else. Then you'll be able to skip ahead a grade, too.

I don't really want to skip ahead.

Having the same teacher and the same classmates all the time. Don't you feel trapped? Abigail says. But joining the older grades wouldn't change anything. Teachers are teachers, and even if I get away from Jaden, some other kid will decide they hate me just like him.

It was still raining at the end of class. Peering out from
a spot I'd cleared in the foggy bus window with my finger, I
saw Mr. O'Neal on his bicycle. He was wearing a raincoat,
and his front basket was empty. Abigail once told me that
hornbills were vulnerable to cold, so he must have left it at
home, where it could stay warm.

When I grow up, I want to be an adventurer and travel
around the world.

I've been on only nine trips in my whole life. Every New
Year break, we go visit the town where Gramma lives, who's
Mom's mom, and stay for a few days. That's the only place
I've ever been. I want to go to the ocean, and the lakes, and
the mountains. But Mom and Dad are both so busy, it's hard
to find time.

"I'll take you away soon. I promise," Mom says, but she's
never kept it.

Sometimes, I get out a big book from the shelf and look at
the photos of auroras, and salt lakes, and deserts, and coral
reefs. When I look at photos of things I've never seen with
my own eyes I feel a contentment like my heart is off somewhere far away, drifting.

When I was in second grade, I ran away from home to try
to get somewhere else.

I packed my backpack with some jerky and a couple of
two-day-old rolls, plus a water bottle, chapstick, a flashlight, and a pocketknife, and waited for Dad and Mom to
fall asleep before sneaking out of the house. I was scared

about someone catching me walking through town before I reached the Andersons' place, but the streets were dead quiet and I didn't see a single soul.

It was summer. There was a lukewarm breeze and the night was still warm enough to make me sweat. Somewhere, an owl hooted. Each time I heard the flap of bird wings, or a dog howling, I froze for a second.

A light was on at the Andersons'. A pack of cats prowled around in the dark. Gramma Anderson herded cats. When she walked through town during the day, a couple dozen of them would appear and follow her around. Mom tells me to stay away, because stray cats are dirty, but I love cats, and secretly kept up with Gramma Anderson.

I asked her once why they followed her.

She laughed heartily, like a witch.

"It's because I know their souls."

"How do you do that?"

"Born that way."

"Could I learn to, if I practiced?"

"Oh, you don't wanna do that."

Gramma Anderson brushed me off. Fair enough—I wasn't that interested in their souls.

Trying not to make a sound, I walked past the Andersons' place as far as I could on the other side of the street. I was almost out of town.

But that was as far as I made it. The Andersons' alarm went off, and I was busted. Mr. Anderson came running out holding a glaring big flashlight in one hand and a black metal object in the other. A gun, I thought.

"Don't shoot!" I shouted. "It's Emma. Emma Jackson."

Mr. Anderson shone his light in my face. Then he pressed the black metal thing against me. I felt my heart contract, thinking he'd shoot me dead any second now. There was a sharp beep. Mr. Anderson peered at me.

"What are you doing out here, girlie?"

"I was just trying to get out of town."

"It doesn't seem like an appropriate time of day for a girlie of your age to be out playing."

"I'm not here to play," I said, before I could think.

"All the more reason, then. Now, tell me your address, and I'll give you a ride home."

He put me on his bicycle and took me straight home, where I immediately got the biggest scolding of my life. Mom was crying. Dad had his head in his hand. But the adults are always telling us to fly free, I thought, though I kept my thoughts to myself. I had other things to worry about.

The thing Mr. Anderson was holding wasn't a gun. Guns didn't sound like that. So what was it?

Every fourth Thursday, in the afternoon, I go to the clinic to see Dr. Lopez. When I was five years old, I was in the hospital for about two months with a mystery illness. I had a high fever for days, and after it passed, I started raving and acting strange. They rushed me to the clinic, where they operated on me and confined me to a blank white room for weeks— or so Dad said. According to Mom, the clinic doesn't lock people up. "You were just in a private room, with a nurse because they were worried about your condition."

What's weird is that my memory from that time is totally missing. I don't remember having a fever, or being at the clinic, or acting or saying anything strange. Instead, I was dreaming. I dreamed I traveled somewhere far away. There were endless forests and a huge lake. Herds of strange animals lived by the water, and there were no humans anywhere. I thought I could see buildings in the distance, and I made my way toward them through the tall plants. No matter how long I walked, they never came nearer. Something flew through the air. A big bird. Its plaintive cry seemed to fill the sky.

Dr. Lopez rolled up my sleeve to take my blood. I liked to watch the needle sink into the soft part of the inside of my elbow.

"Not scared?" Dr. Lopez asks.

"No. It's interesting," I say, and he shrugs.

Some tests and some questions. I spend about an hour in Dr. Lopez's clinic. I'll see you next month. Until then—don't let the big bird get you, Dr. Lopez says, and gives me a wink. Before I started grade school, I always laughed when the doctor said this, but now that it's been years, I'm not sure how I should react.

Is that some kind of spell, I asked him once.

That's right, he said. An incantation handed down through my family for generations to ward off evil.

I didn't believe him. I can tell when people are lying to me.

—

Most people lie.

Abigail lies, Mom lies, and so does Dad.

Sometimes they're small lies, and sometimes they're big. But I think things would be pretty hard if there were no more lies in the world. Nick, at the Millars' next door, was always switching girlfriends. Nick lied a lot, and the girls loved it. I asked him about it once.

"How do you remember which lie you tell to which girl?"

Nick looked stunned. "Watch your mouth, kid," he said.

But I knew he wasn't lying to me. So after that, I started talking to him sometimes.

"The girls—do you like them?"

"Yeah, I do."

"What do you like about them?"

"They're nice."

"You're lying."

"Well, yeah. They aren't nice, not a bit."

"Then why do you like them?"

Nick thought about it. "Who knows? Either way, a kid like you wouldn't understand about stuff between men and women," Nick said, and walked off.

He was lying, after all. He didn't like girls at all, and he knew it.

Sometime after that, Nick left town with a girl. The girl got found immediately and brought back home, but Nick was still gone. I liked him quite a lot. When he called me kid, it made me think of the way the wind blew in that faraway land I'd dreamed of.

Gramma Anderson died last week.

It rained the day of the funeral. I went to the cemetery after school, but the funeral was over and there was nobody there, not the pastor or the Andersons or anyone else. I stepped onto the patch of freshly dug and leveled earth. I thought about Gramma Anderson lying under the dirt. What did it feel like when you died? We go to heaven when we die, Mom says. But I didn't believe in heaven.

There were other things I didn't believe, too. What we learned in history class at school, for one. I can't believe all those historical figures ever really existed. I'm sure our teacher wasn't trying to tell us lies, but I just couldn't imagine the people in my history textbooks living, speaking, eating meals, and going out with girls like Nick did, or kissing boys like Abigail.

"You're funny, Emma," Abigail says, and laughs. "But those are some pretty free ideas."

You're wrong, I think, but this is something I don't think even Abigail, my best friend, would understand. I'm not free at all. I'm always trapped, in a blank white room, like Dad said.

The cemetery was full of cats. I crouched down and tried meowing at a black cat, but it ignored me. Now that Gramma Anderson was dead, who was going to feed all these cats? The footprints of dozens of cats tracked haphazardly across the soft soil.

—

Jaden was coming for me.

It was over nothing. Jaden had told the teacher such an obvious lie as an excuse for having forgotten his homework that I couldn't help but laugh a little inside.

I didn't show it on my face, but somehow Jaden knew. It was amazing how sensitive they were, these people who hated me. They were amazingly responsive to my every move.

After class, Jaden kept hovering around me. Even though it was a Wednesday, Abigail had been called out by a teacher, and I had no one on my side. As I started to try to get away, Jaden sped up and chased. I ran but Jaden was faster. Right when I knew he was going to get me, he reached out and grabbed my hair and yanked me toward him. The pain was unbelievable. I yelled for help but there was nobody there. Jaden was cunning. It was the music room, where I always ate lunch on rainy days precisely because no one ever used it.

Jaden hit me. In the gut, on the cheek, in my chest. I curled up on the floor. I threw up. Jaden was laughing. My eyes swam with tears. Not out of sadness, but from sheer misery. I hated him. I knew I shouldn't hate him, but right then, it was impossible not to.

A flash of bright light filled the room.

Jaden collapsed.

Why was Mr. Anderson here, instead of a teacher, I wondered, vaguely. Mr. Anderson bent down over Jaden, who was slumped on the floor, and checked whether he was breathing. "Can you hear me?" he said, but Jaden didn't respond.

Mr. Anderson lifted up Jaden's body, with zero effort, and was about to leave the music room. Just as he got to the door, he turned around.

"Clear that sick up," he said.

"Wait."

"What now?"

"Is Jaden okay?"

With Jaden in his arms, Mr. Anderson shrugged. Like he'd said that night, he said, "You'd know better than me, wouldn't you, girlie?"

I didn't know anything. Wait—was that true? I hadn't laid a finger on him. But the sensation was familiar.

Once Mr. Anderson left, everything went eerily quiet. Almost like there was nobody else left in the whole school. There was no sound of the bell, or chatter of students. I opened the music room window and the wind rushed in. There was no one on the street. I stood there for a while, and Mr. O'Neal rode across on his bicycle—the birdcage in his basket just as usual.

I woke up in the night.

Mom and Dad were arguing. The two of them fought sometimes—always in the middle of the night, when I was supposed to be asleep.

When I peeked through the doorway on my way back from the bathroom, they were still arguing. I listened in. I can't do it anymore, Mom said. She scares me.

How can you say that? She's our child. You birthed her yourself, Dad said.

They were fighting about me. I wanted to cry. I saw the way Mom looked. I knew that look. It was the same as when Jaden hated me.

I crept back to my room silently. I pulled the covers over my head to muffle my crying. I didn't get any more sleep that night.

I knew where I had to go.

I couldn't stay in this town any longer. I had to leave and go somewhere far away.

I'd pretended not to know it, but everyone had always hated me.

Not just Jaden, but my teachers and classmates, and Mom, and—though I didn't want to admit it—even Abigail.

Everyone but Dad, maybe. He'd never looked at me with that same hateful expression, at least. But that was all. Not hating me was still totally different from loving me.

I got ready to leave and did a much better job of it than I had when I was in second grade. Underwear, some changes of clothes. My diary and a few photos. A necklace Mom had bought me and a music box that was a present from Dad. I wanted to bring some food, too, but the kitchen was right next to Mom and Dad's room, so I decided against it.

At dawn, I silently pushed open the front door and stepped outside. It smelled like winter. A bird was crying.

The sidewalk was covered in dead leaves. I turned to look at my house, just once, and never looked back.

Just like last time, there was a light on in the Andersons' place. Several cats were prowling around the house.

After a while, Mr. Anderson came outside.

"You're going for real this time," he said. He was holding a long, dark, metallic thing in his hand.

"Is Jaden dead?"

"No, he made it. You had enough sense to pull back before you crossed the line."

"But nobody likes me now. Not even Mom or Dad."

"If only our gramma was still here."

"But she's dead."

I didn't belong here. I was as human as they were, but I could never be one of them.

"Our gramma liked this town. She had her cats, too."

"Sure. Unlike her, not even the cats want to be my friend."

Mr. Anderson gave me a faint smile.

"Gramma's power only worked on cats. Same goes for me. But you're different, girlie. Your power is stronger by far."

I didn't want a power like that.

"But you're our great hope," Mr. Anderson said.

That's a lie, I thought. I wasn't anyone's hope. As soon as I left this town, everybody would forget all about me. Would try to forget all about me.

"Your mom who bore you will remember you. So will your dad," Mr. Anderson said, with a little pity.

From the other end of the street, I hear the sound of Mr. O'Neal's bicycle approaching. The big hornbill's cage is in its front basket. Mr. Anderson touched the black metal stick to my chest. I heard a voice say, *Delete.* I no longer existed in this town. Mr. O'Neal rode right up to me.

"Shall we?" The voice came from the hornbill, not Mr. O'Neal.

"Who are you?" I asked the bird.

"Wotcher," it replied.

Without a word, Mr. O'Neal opened the door of the cage. The hornbill flapped lightly and took off into the sky, moving its wings in wide arcs. I started running, following it away from the edge of town and deeper into the woods.

| Echoes |

"Why a bird?" Jakob sometimes asks.

My answer is always: "So I can fly. And see in the dark."

Jakob O'Neal is my watch partner in this town. Normally, a watcher keeps watch alone, but we work as a pair.

Jakob is well-liked by everyone here. When he goes around town on his bicycle with the hornbill riding in his front basket, many of the residents call out to him, and Jakob responds to each one. To excitable old Mr. Greenwood, he smiles and says hello as he rides past. With Mrs. Hathaway, who won't let you get a word in edgewise for at least five minutes once she starts talking, he dismounts and listens, nodding patiently after every sentence. And when the children ride past on the fossil-fuel school bus, he always waves at them with a smile.

Once the round is done, Jakob heads for home. Our small cottage is just outside town, in the other direction from the Andersons' house. Jakob takes the hornbill's cage and puts it next to me where I lie in the easy chair. I unsync from the hornbill and transfer my consciousness back to my own body.

"Time for coffee," Jakob says, and puts the water on to boil while he grinds the beans. He lets the grounds bloom and then slowly pours the rest of the hot water over them.

"A cup of coffee in the morning, another in the afternoon, and one more at night," he says, and drinks it contentedly.

Jakob was never a coffee drinker in the old days. When he had to, he always ordered decaf. He wouldn't have dreamed of brewing it for himself.

We were so busy back then.

"I hope Emma's getting used to life over at the research center," he said, putting his cup down on the table. Emma had just recently needed to leave the town. If only her mother had been a different type, she might have been able to stay a little longer—but her mother had become afraid of her, so it was time for her to go. Children could survive trouble with school friends and teachers as long as their parents protected them, but once the family became fearful, that was usually the end.

"I'm sure she is."

"Poor child."

"We did everything we could for her."

I thought about all the children who had left over the years.

Noah, Lidia, Cristian, Isaac, and Aubree. Each of them had some ability that set them apart. Lidia was clairvoyant.

Cristian and Isaac had exceptional IQs, and Aubree had a latent affinity for fire. When the town hall burned down, that was because of Aubree; but the fault had been the townspeople's for making Aubree angry. The fire was what you might call a natural consequence.

"Ian," Jakob said. "Do you notice your memories getting less vivid lately?"

The sunlight was strong for a winter day. On our last watch round, lines of laundry had festooned the front gardens of the houses along the streets.

"No, not for me."

"I seem to be having some trouble recalling things. Things from before." Jakob sighed and put his coffee cup down on the table again. The wooden surface was covered in marks. I always told him not to put hot drinks straight on the table, and he never listened.

"Before? Which before do you mean?"

"I'm talking about back when we started. That before."

"You mean the first you and me."

In my mind's eye I saw, from earlier that day, a sudden gust of wind overturn a bedsheet pegged on the line outside the mayor's house. Our memories, Jakob's and mine, reached far back into the past—through dozens of generations of the two of us.

Watchers came in several different types.

It was Jakob and I who—based on urgent data collection and research, taking into consideration the conditions and environment in each region, and with the full-scale cooperation of the mothers—had identified and installed the individuals who would watch over each region.

As a result of multiple impacts and other catastrophic events, the human population was in free fall. We were on the brink of population collapse. The question we faced was how to preserve even a slim chance that we might someday thrive on this planet again. Across the world, we brought together the foremost intellects, unearthed every old technology that might have some application, ran lengthy calculations on our computers, and found not a single way through.

"No moves left. This might be our cue to bow out."

I've never forgotten the sound of Jakob's voice as he said this—Jakob O'Neal, a man who had never resigned himself to anything.

"Humans have been saying that for a long time now."

"To be sure. The difference being they never really believed it back then."

"Maybe you're right."

"How else could they have carried on spreading war and famine and pollution like they did for quite so long? Talk about hubris!"

It had sounded to me then like Jakob was giving up entirely. But I misunderstood him.

Jakob came up with a plan: a radical plan that provided the blueprint for the survival of *Homo sapiens* in its current form.

The plan wouldn't have merited a second look if our circumstances had been even slightly less desperate. But by then, there was no one left who would resist or even criticize it.

Many nations had already vanished. Those that still remained were barely functioning as states. Jakob's plan was a last resort: an option that had, by then, ceased to be a choice.

Communities of humans would be separated into a number of regions and isolated from one another completely. Watchers would be placed in each region to maintain continuous observation over the population. All reproductive taboos would be lifted, while mechanisms of competition would be managed carefully in order to mitigate the effects of survival of the fittest and preserve as much genetic diversity as possible.

Putting the plan in place had been straightforward, given that the greater part of human religion, philosophy, and ideology had already been lost.

"Wind's picking up," Jakob muttered, bringing in T-shirts and a raincoat from the line.

"Good weather for flying."

Once again, I synced my consciousness with the hornbill, which had left its cage and was flapping lightly around the room. Birds are capricious. Even compared with dogs or cats, they lack focus. When I spent too long synced to the bird, I felt my nature change a little, too.

"Are you headed to the woods?" Jakob asked.

On sunny days, I usually spent a few hours among the trees.

"That's the plan."

"I'll never get used to it."

"To what?"

"Hearing your voice come out of that bird."

I know Jakob isn't talking about how he feels about me syncing to other creatures. He just finds it unnerving to hear our pet hornbill talking like a human.

"Really? We've been doing this with the animals for a few years now."

"You always dig up the strangest tek."

It's true I enjoy searching through old files. I found this method of implanting a bird with an artificial larynx in a document from around eight thousand years ago.

"All I do is dig them up from the archive. You know humans have been coming up with peculiar ideas forever."

I love flying through the forest as a bird. The topsoil that harbors so many organisms. Colonies of deciduous broadleafs. Conifers that stay bushy and blue-green all winter. Novel gymnosperms emerging from long, slow ecological transitions. And the panoply of different fauna.

Winged insects of all sizes—impossible to perceive clearly while I'm in human form—tempt me with their sweet scent. The bright wingbeats of hummingbirds make music only birds can hear. A medium-size carnivore stalks onto a patch of grass, and by reflex I take flight into the open skies above the canopy. The inexpressible primitive fear of that moment.

"Ian Chen," Jakob says, smiling. "Don't go getting eaten up out there now."

I've been captured by predators several times while synced to an animal. The agony and torment of being devoured was

part of my memory forever now. That, along with the blissful
cessation of awareness that follows.

I perched on the thick trunk of the dawn redwood and rested
my wings, and thought about Emma, the last child to have
left our town.

Emma had been brave. Many kids felt overwhelmed by
their individuality, but not her. Jakob and I had kept a close
eye on her since she was just a toddler. She'd barely been able
to get her mouth to form the name *Mr. O'Neal*, but she'd
been aware of the scope of her ability even then.

Normally, children like to show off what they can do:
Brush their teeth. Use a knife. Go on errands for their
mother. Sing all three verses of a song. Run fast. But Emma
never let anyone see that she could move things without
touching them, or feel what others felt, or predict what was
about to happen. She knew these abilities made her different.

Children bearing transformative potential appeared in
the community somewhere in the order of once every several hundred years. Emma's variation showed signs of being
especially powerful.

"We'll need to think about when to get her out of here."

Jakob and I kept thinking. We drew comparisons with
past data and reran the statistics. There was always the option to keep a variant individual in the community and seed
a minute genetic difference across the entire group. The natural human attachment to the place of one's birth couldn't
be discounted.

Emma was growing up. Jakob and I were torn. She was smart. Couldn't we find a way to let her stay?

In the end, it didn't work out.

"Humans," Jakob said. He was perversely impressed. "It seems you can always count on them to sniff out what doesn't belong."

"You can say that again. I still don't understand why they have to be so intolerant of change."

"Are you sure, Ian?"

Jakob looked at me. For a moment, I quailed. Several remembered scenes rose briefly to my mind before fading again.

"I guess it depends." My blood felt hot. Too hot.

I'd made a mistake.

Even so, at the time, Jakob didn't reproach me at all.

It took a few hundred years after the regions were isolated from one another for the first mutant to turn up in our town. When it did, it took us by surprise.

One morning, Jakob said, "I've been having these odd dreams."

"What are they like?" I asked. I was aware of my heart beating in my chest.

"I'd call them nightmares."

"Of what?"

Jakob didn't answer. If his dreams were like the ones I was having, he couldn't have described them if he'd tried.

"I don't want to talk about it."

They weren't the kind of nightmares that just scared you. They showed you the darkest, ugliest parts of yourself and left you feeling raw. And as much as I despised the acts and scenes that laid bare my own flawed nature, they also brought a kind of sticky gratification. I'd wake from the darkness at my own cries and find with relief that I was only dreaming. But I would also feel dismay at the dream being cut short, at finding myself cast back out into my own clean bed.

"I've been having them all the time, too. The nightmares."

"You have, have you?" Jakob's eyes met mine, and they looked hollow.

Jakob was slowly getting sicker. His appetite was worse, he was getting thin; his energy was fading. I had to sync myself into his body to get our watch rounds done.

It was only by sheer chance that we found the boy. According to the town records, he didn't exist. Both Jakob and I knew everyone who lived in our town, from the newborn to the old, sick, and dying.

"Hey!"

As soon as the boy spotted us—me synced to Jakob's body—he cried out, and stopped, and stared.

I couldn't have described the expression on his face. A complicated mixture of admiration, hate, contempt, awe—

"Where have you come from?" I asked him.

He didn't answer. Only later did we find out that the boy had been born in secret to an unwed teen, the granddaughter of the town mayor. No one knew who the father was, and the child had been brought up hidden in a barn on the mayor's property.

"Over that way," the boy said, and pointed east. "I know all about you," he said. Too artlessly.

I glared at him. His knowing tone rubbed me the wrong way.

"I can see inside your heart," he said. I said nothing, kept my eyes on him. "You know, out of everyone in this town, your nightmares are the worst."

"How do you—" I asked, without thinking.

"I freed all your minds so you could stop pretending!"

In that moment, I realized the boy was a mutant.

"Tell me how you learned to do that," I said, trying to draw him out.

"Don't use that voice on me. I know what you're thinking, remember? I know how cold your heart is."

As soon as the boy said this, a torrent of nightmare fragments came rushing into my mind. I clutched my head.

"So it was you that made the world this way," he said with glee.

"You don't know what you're saying!" I said. I was shouting.

The boy shrugged. "Of course I do. I hate it here. Truly. This whole world's full of fakes, you can't breathe, and nothing ever changes. You think so too, don't you? That's why I'm going to break it all apart."

I understood then what this boy could do. He would probe into the deepest undercurrents of the minds and memories of everyone in our town and let loose what he found.

I synced to him. Compounding a sync was terribly risky, but I didn't hesitate. As soon as the link was established, the child's consciousness came rushing into my mind—a whirlpool of memories from everyone in the town, churning and rearing and forming into pure chaos, filling me up.

With Jakob's arms, I picked up a rock from the ground. I drove it against the boy's head. A staggering pain assaulted me through the sync, but I bore it without letting go.

I could feel the boy's consciousness fading, along with the part of mine that was synced to him. The wound wasn't fatal, but the boy was trying to slip away. *No. Stay*, I said.

"As a species, we simply don't have what it takes," Jakob had said. His voice sounded strained.

This was before we were clones, back when we were humans born by normal biological reproduction, shortly before Jakob's plan was put into place. More than five thousand years ago now.

"The decline of humankind can't be stopped—not by you, or me, or anyone else on the planet. None of us has the power," he said. "We were supposed to be so much more than this."

I looked at him. He looked back at me steadily.

"I've got to make a different kind of human."

I took a sharp breath. "Artificially?"

"To some extent, yes. But in the end—no."

"Then how?"

"Evolution."

"What do you mean?"

"In the past, when people were abundant on earth, human traffic on a large scale prevented the genetic separation necessary for evolutionary processes to take hold. But things have changed. There are so few of us left. This is our opportunity. While we still have the numbers. And some understanding of the knowledge and technology. First, we secure immediate genetic isolation. Pile on extreme stress, drastic environmental change. We provoke mutations on a far shorter timescale than in any previous evolutionary process."

"Stress and environmental change? What are you talking about, Jakob? Isn't that exactly what we've been subjected to for years? What more do you think you can do?"

Jakob looked at me. "Ian, do you think you're a good person?"

"Do I what?"

"Think you're a good person. I don't think I am. Or perhaps I should say . . . I don't believe in myself."

I understood what he meant, and I hated it. Like he said, it had become impossible for human beings to trust ourselves. Our history was full of enough contradictions to destroy any sense of self-belief. As a species we were like an octopus trying to survive by eating its own limbs. And while we all saw the fatal error we were making, no one stepped forward with a decisive solution. Some tried, but their efforts had done as much good as a dropperful of water in the ocean.

"So we'll fade out. Make space for the ones who come next."

I wanted to scream. But there was no help coming. What Jakob was suggesting seemed insane, but what humanity had done to itself and to the planet was even worse.

"I look at you, Ian, and it gives me just a little hope," Jakob said. He came over and stood in front of my easy chair and carefully touched my motionless arms, my unmoving legs. "What you can do . . . it's a sign of what we could become."

"You're talking about syncing."

The fact that I, while having been born without the use of my limbs, was able to merge my consciousness with that of other living beings was a secret known only to my parents, Jakob, and a few others.

"That's it. What's more, I have much more confidence in you than I do in myself."

"Why?"

"Who knows? It's just a hunch." Jakob laughed. It was a windy day. It was summer.

I brought the unconscious boy back to the cottage and laid his slender body on the sofa. Then, slowly and carefully, I unlinked from Jakob.

He looked at the boy in surprise. "What's this?"

"I lost my head."

I told Jakob what had happened that day. How I'd had to weigh up the value of a variant against the danger of an individual who would destroy the entire system on which our world was built. And how, in that split second, I'd picked the option that preserved the world that Jakob had created.

But maybe what I told him was just an excuse I came up with after the fact. Maybe I'd simply acted out of fear.

The boy seemed to me to be a fundamentally alien being. I'd always known, of course, that those who knew about my own ability feared me, too—some more, some less. But I, in turn, had felt threatened by the boy.

My instinct had been unable to tolerate what was different in him.

I couldn't hold others to a standard that I'd failed to meet myself. I'd learned that much, at least.

Both Jakob and I paid close attention to the variants that appeared after the boy. To just how much we, and those around them, were able to accept their alienness.

"That boy there—he said he knew what was in my mind?" Jakob had asked.

"That's what he said. Everything."

"Ian, do you think it was *my* mind he saw into? Or yours, in my body?"

I gave it some thought. Jakob waited.

"I expect it was both of us."

The boy survived. He stayed with us at the cottage for several weeks, until his wounds were fully healed, and then left our town. We gave him a name. They'd been so afraid of him that they'd never even named him.

On his last night, Jakob and I threw him a party. We'd hardly come to understand each other during the time he was with us, but the mood that evening was warm and cordial.

Jakob baked the boy a cake and wrote the name we'd given him, Noah, in icing on top. The boy looked at it and blinked. It was the most childlike I'd ever seen him look.

Jakob and I both slept through the night for the first time in weeks.

—

The forest is lively as always. Tiny fricative insect noises. The gay chatter of birds. Minute sounds of plants growing. Different waters trickling as they circulate.

In the late afternoon, I fly back to the cottage and am surprised to find Jakob asleep on the couch.

I stay synced to the hornbill until it gets back on the perch inside its cage, and then uncouple.

"Good morning." I smile at Jakob, who opens his eyes.

"Fell asleep, did I? It must be getting on for patrol time."

"Not just yet."

"Time for coffee, then."

Jakob gets to his feet heavily. This Jakob is getting old. They found a small cancerous mass in his kidney two years ago. He's being treated with immunotherapy. We know, from the data, that Jakob's body is prone to tumors. We also know, from the data, that the prognosis is better without surgery.

"Jakob. Did you say some of the memories are going?" I ask.

"That they are," Jakob says, letting the coffee bloom.

"We've accumulated quite a few over the years."

"Five millenia's worth, and change."

"Stands to reason we'd lose some along the way."

"They're not lost. Just—fading."

"You're sure about that?"

"So I am."

It was nearly sunset. The wind had stilled, and the cold was settling. Clear winter days were always like this.

Clonal humans don't normally retain memories from the original body. Just like infants created by natural reproduction, they're new bodies, with freshly wiped memories. Jakob and I were unusual in retaining our generational memories. Ever since this trait came to light, we've generated clones not from our preserved originals, or any of several intermediate generations, but from cells of the most recent specimen body. As a result, we both remember everything of significance to happen in the last five thousand years.

"How old do you think you'll get this time around?"

"Going by the average, I expect to have a few more years." Jakob pours the coffee into his cup. "You've got a while to go, Ian."

I nod.

Through accidental deaths and natural differences in life span, our ages had drifted closer and farther apart over the years.

"I still wonder what happened to Noah after he left."

As watchers, we have no involvement with the children after they leave our town. That, too, was part of the plan.

"Tell me, Ian—which memories feel the most real to you?" Jakob asks.

I take a while to think.

"Right now," I say, "the ones from this me."

The hornbill cries out sharply, like a screw turning. The sun has set. Jakob takes his cup over to the sink. I gaze at the rings on the tabletop and search through my memory for murmurs of forest streams, voices of birds. Sounds from the day settle to rest gently over sounds I heard a thousand years ago, echoing through my mind.

| *The Lake* |

8 of 15.

That's my name.

I have three brothers and two sisters. My brothers' names are 3 of 15, 5 of 15, and 6 of 15. My sisters are 4 of 15 and 7 of 15. I had another sister, 2 of 15, but she got sick and died a little after 4 was born.

My other siblings are all grown up now, and my brothers 3, 5, and 6 have already left home. 5 lives alone near the forest, and 3 and 6 both live with their wives.

7 and I aren't married yet, but 4 got a husband some time ago. He lives with her here, and they're expecting a child soon.

Now that my brothers have left home, I hardly see them

except at New Year, when they come back home for three days. They're busy working hard to raise their children and provide for their families.

We gathered for New Year just recently.

When the Lake freezes over, and the ice gets thick, and the cold deepens, and the surface of the ice starts rising in the dead of night, then it's New Year.

It's the women's job to take the precious flour made from the store of grain that was harvested at the end of the summer and knead it with leaven made from lavender and honey to bake the bread. It's the men's job to cook the birds that have been hanging since autumn and the salt-packed fish. My brother 5 was especially skilled at this. He was good with herbs and knew more of the mushroom spots in the forest than anybody else in the village.

I always asked 5 to show me where the mushrooms grew, but he never would.

"That's a secret I keep from everyone, even Mother and Father," he said.

"Then what will happen if you die?"

"Somebody else will find them eventually."

"But what will we do for mushrooms until then?"

"You can't get greedy. Don't you think mushrooms need time to rest, too?" 5 said, smiling.

What did he mean by rest?

"Women can't always be bearing children, either, can they? It's like that."

5 had three children with three different women.

If a man lives on his own without taking a wife, his children live with their mother until around the age of three. After that, they can go back and forth between the father and the mother and choose where they prefer to live.

5's children loved him, so they had been with him for a long time now. They were all good kids, and we got on well together. I think that was because I got along well with 5. Sometimes, you didn't get along with people, even if they were your brothers or sisters. This hadn't happened yet in my family, but at the house of 22, which was nearby, there had been two conflicts just in the last ten years. The first one was when 3 of 22 was struck by 4 of 22, and the second one was when 15 of 22 was struck by 13 of 22.

When 3 of 22 was attacked, that was before I was old enough to know what happened. I was visiting 22 when 15 of 22 was attacked. 13 of 22 was a big man, and he and his brother 15 of 22 always went about together and often wrestled each other more roughly than normal. But wrestling and fighting were very different things.

The women of the neighborhood said the two of them had disagreed over a woman.

At that time, everyone in the village held a meeting, and 13 of 22 was banished for a year. The discussion focused on the presence or absence of hate within 13 of 22. In the end, it was proved from the testimony of many witnesses, and from questioning 13 of 22 himself, that there had been no hate present in the wrestling that 13 of 22 and 15 of 22 had habitually engaged in, so 13 of 22 avoided being sent away forever.

13 of 22 was back in the village and was now married. His wife is not the woman who they said was the reason for the disagreement between 13 of 22 and 15 of 22.

I was right there when 15 of 22 was struck. I've never seen anything so frightening. 13 of 22's face was contorted, and his body gave off ripples of something like electricity. I didn't see it, exactly, but I could feel it was there.

My brother 5 doesn't live with a woman, but my brothers 3 and 6 have wives that they live with. So 3's and 6's children don't have any half siblings.

It's forbidden for two siblings, or a parent and child, to have sex. That includes half siblings. Of course, most people would never have desires of that kind. But my mother said that unless you were careful, sometimes sex could happen between close relatives by accident.

"If you live together, there's nothing to worry about. You wouldn't want to do that with 3 or 5 or 6, would you?"

I shook my head. I haven't had sex yet. Secretly, though, there was a boy that I thought about touching, kissing, and laying my head against.

"I can't imagine doing anything like that with any of my brothers," I said, laughing.

"No. But sometimes children feel that way." My mother frowned.

"Why would they do such a thing?"

I love my brothers, of course, but only in the same way that I love my mother, my father, and the flowers in the forest.

It's a totally different love from the kind where you pine after them, and can't stop thinking about them.

"Sometimes, if you grow up without seeing very much of a parent or a sibling, and meet them for the first time after you're grown, you fall in love by accident," my mother said.

"Okay."

"Maybe because they're . . . both like you and not like you. That's why you love them."

My mother looked a little sad. I didn't know the reason then—it wasn't until a little while later that I found out that she had been in love with her half brother, but they weren't able to be together.

There's a big book that is kept in the village chief's house.

Its pages are covered in formal script, written using a quill and ink made of soot. Only the chief's family can read the formal script. The other villagers and I can read and write, but we know only the simplified script.

The chief's house is the house of 1, and the chief is called 1 of 1.

The chief is decided by vote, not by heredity. They learn how to read when they become chief. The children born in the chief's house also learn. So aside from the chief, there's a handful of people in the village that can also read the big book.

The current chief—or, if the chief has died, one of their sons or daughters—usually wins the vote. So although in theory the position isn't hereditary, it's very rare that someone from a different lineage is chosen to be chief. Our current chief has been the chief since I was born, by being elected every five years.

I've been told that the lineage of chiefs has changed just once since our village was founded. It was because they failed to prevent a great fire in the village. When I learned about this, I thought how they must have hated turning from 1 of 1 into 1 of nothing. The chief who wasn't able to prevent the fire went to live at the edge of the village but disappeared after some time. Their lineage has also died out now.

The book in the chief's house is a record of the history of the village.

The village was founded by 1 of 1 and 2 of 1. They were husband and wife and had six children between them. The village gradually grew from there, and at one time there were so many people that we couldn't all fit on this headland. But the head count was reduced by disease and famine and fire and harbor waves, then recovered, and fell again, and grew again, and so on. Now, around five hundred of us live in the village and its surroundings. Our population has been pretty stable for the last several hundred years.

Our days are full.

The village feeds itself through farming and hunting, but the only things that hunting gets are small birds; bigger prey are very rare. When the village was first started, there was the occasional boar or deer, but they soon disappeared.

Recently, though, the men have caught a few rats and rabbits, and each of these is an occasion to celebrate.

We catch more fish than birds. The Lake fish are small, and the sea fish are bigger. The men swim into the water to fish. Of the food the sea gives us, my favorite is hurcheon. When I crack open its shell and suck on the orange stuff inside, my mouth fills up with its sweetness.

Of my siblings, my brother 6 is the best fisher. Since he left home, we don't have fish every day, but when he gets a big catch, 6 will send his wife 20 of 36 back with a share for us.

20 of 36 brings us a basket of fish and chats with my mother, or me, or my sister 7. 20 of 36 is in love with my brother 6.

"I'm so happy every day. I can't tell you how happy I am," 20 of 36 says, dreamily. She says she doesn't have eyes for any other men. And 6 apparently feels the same.

"8, do you think you'd like to get married like 6 and 20 of 36?" my sister 7 asked me, after 20 of 36 left. I thought about it.

"I'm not sure. I mean, I haven't even had sex yet."

7 put the palm of her hand on my head and gave me a pat.

"I don't want to get married. I want to stay free, like 5's lovers, and go out hunting and fishing," 7 said, looking out into the distance.

My sister 7 had always been adventurous and was good at climbing trees and catching insects. Roasted crickets were my favorite treat.

—

There had been several mass deaths in the history of the village.

There was a periodic plague that would spread when there were too many hot days in a summer. It gave you a high fever and made you unable to keep food down, until your skin and muscle and bones were all worn out.

The plague had light years and heavy years. In light years, hardly anyone died. In heavy ones, which came once every few hundred years, it killed whole flocks of birds and insects as well as people. 5 said the plague was the reason we never saw larger animals near the village.

"How do you know that?" I asked him.

"I heard it from 44 of 1, at the chief's house," he said.

44 of 1 had always been fond of 5. She was very beautiful and had two children. One of them, 11 of 1, was good friends with 5.

"The very first 1 of 1 and 2 of 1 had survived the plague," 5 said. "There used to be many, many more people, but the plague killed most of them. And the animals dropped like flies, too."

"Huh," I said.

Many, many more people. How many could there have been? Around the same number as when the village was at its largest, a little more than two thousand?

"Hundreds of thousands," 5 said, as if that was nothing.

That many people? I didn't think it could be true. 5 had to be lying. He loved to play tricks on me.

—

My mother said we love people when they are both like us and not like us.

But I felt like the people of the village were all a little alike. The main way they were the same was that nobody hated anyone.

"What is hate, anyway?" I asked my mother.

"It means you wish something would disappear from the world," my mother said.

I thought immediately of 13 of 22.

The electric charge that had rippled off 13 of 22's body in the conflict between him and 15 of 22. Could that be something that was made when you hated someone?

But it had been determined that there was no element of hate involved when 13 of 22 struck 15 of 22.

"Have you ever seen anyone with hate?" I asked my mother.

"Never," she said.

"I wonder what it would feel like."

"I don't know," she said, but her face clouded over, just a little. It was the way she looked when she was holding in something she wanted to say.

I wondered if she knew something about hate. But I didn't ask her any more about it.

19 of 30 was an unusual kid. His house was right by the Lake.

I liked 19 of 30. I was probably a little in love with him— but maybe not passionately so.

19 of 30 lived with his mother, 11 of 30. He wasn't sure who his father was.

"25 of 19, or 17 of 51, or 7 of 86, or maybe 50 of 3, according to Mom," said 19 of 30, telling me the names of the men who might be his father.

"You've never lived with your father?"

"Nope."

We were fishing in the Lake. 19 of 30 had taken three fish, and I had one.

"Do you want to?"

"Not really."

19 of 30's mother, 11 of 30, had left home when he was born, even though she was a woman, choosing to live on her own by the shore of the Lake.

Women who had children, either without or with marrying a man, usually stayed in the house where they were born. And if her child, past the age of three, eventually chose to stay with their father, she would remain in the house she was born into and work for the household. Both women and men had to work hard to live. Cooking, farming. Washing and cleaning. Preserving. Chopping wood. Sewing and getting water.

It wasn't easy living as just two—especially when one was only a child.

"But we have fun," 19 of 30 would say with a smile.

Their house was modest, and when I visited there wasn't much to eat. In our village, it's customary to welcome visitors with a spread of food, but they were so poor that it was all they had.

"Don't you get hungry?"

"Sometimes. But I don't mind. We're free, Mother and me."

Free is a word that 19 of 30 sometimes uses. I'm not really sure what it means, in the same way that I don't know about *hate*.

Everyone in the village has their own name.

For example, my house is the house of 15, and I'm 8 of 15.

There are a hundred houses in the village. Children take the number of their mother's house. My mother's mother was from 15, so she's 1 of 15. And my father is 48 of 7, because his mother was from the house of 7.

Within a family line, children are given numbers in rising order, no matter who their mother is. So children with lots of cousins aren't named the number that comes right after their older sibling. My house is unusual because my mother had no siblings, and her cousins are much older, too. Most houses have lots of cousins and aunts and uncles, all living together in a happy muddle.

First numbers end at 50. After 50, the names start over at 1: if 1's still alive, then it's 2; if 2's alive too, then 3, or the next open number.

In the village, our names don't change from when we're born until we die, except for the village chief. If somebody other than the old chief becomes chief, then the new chief leaves their name and becomes 1 of 1. And if they have a husband or a wife, then their spouse become 2 of 1.

The people of the village usually live around forty years.

Many die while they're still young, from illness. It's very rare to have a house where only one person has died, like my sister. For example, my mother lost so many of her siblings that she's the only one left.

It was better for men and women from houses of the same number to avoid having sex, even if they weren't siblings, or parent and child. But that wasn't necessarily a rule that always had to be followed.

I talked about a lot of things with 19 of 30.

About yesterdays, for instance.

The day before yesterday was the day before yesterday. The day before that was the day before yesterday's yesterday. And before that? How far did they go? That was the kind of thing 19 of 30 would say.

If you followed them—from yesterday, to the day before yesterday, to the day before that—the yesterdays would take you all the way back to when the village was founded.

"But what about the day before that? What kind of day do you think that would have been?" 19 of 30 wondered.

I told him what my brother 5 had told me: that a long time before the village was here, there were hundreds of thousands of people, many different large animals, and people living in other lands, not just the headland where the village was.

"But that could have just been one of 5's jokes," I added.

"I think it was true," 19 of 30 said. Raptly, he went on, "Other lands. I wish I could see them."

"Please don't leave," I cried out, to my own surprise.

I didn't want to leave the village and go somewhere new. I loved my house and life in our village.

"I won't," 19 of 30 said. "Don't worry." Gently, he put his arm around my shoulders. I leaned my head against his chest. I felt like I was dreaming.

We stayed there by the Lake together until sunset.

19 of 30 and I talked about tomorrows, too.

"How far do you think tomorrow of tomorrow of tomorrow goes?" he said.

"Until we die," I said, but 19 of 30 shook his head.

"7 of 30's dead, but we still have tomorrows."

But that's—I almost said, before I stopped myself. After some time, I said, carefully, "You still have your tomorrow. But what happened to 7 of 30's tomorrows?"

"Oh, yeah," 19 of 30 said, and looked at me. "There were no more tomorrows for 7 of 30."

"Yeah."

"So there are all different tomorrows. Mine, yours, Mother's, and all my maybe fathers'."

"I think that must be right."

Over the Lake, it started to rain. It wet my body and my hair. It had been cold for a while, but the days were slowly warming.

"Are you warm enough?" 19 of 30 asked and drew me toward him.

"I am now."

"Don't you wish all my tomorrows and all your tomorrows could be together like this? Tomorrow, and the day after that, and the day after that, and on and on?"

"Yeah."

The sun was shining on the Lake through the rain. If only we could stay, I thought. But we had to head home soon. There was work to do in the field, and dinner to cook.

"I have to go," I said, getting up.

19 of 30 hugged me tightly for a second before we kissed for the first time.

"I've been sensing strange signs lately."

My brother 5, who was home for the first time in a while, was telling our mother and father.

"Signs?" our father asked.

"When I'm out walking in the forest, I sense things I never usually feel."

"I haven't noticed anything," our father said, shrugging. "But we're getting bigger animals lately, that's for sure," he said, and grinned.

Since the New Year, we had been catching bigger and bigger animals. So much that we were running out of salt to preserve them. Just recently, they had trapped a four-legged animal with sharp teeth that no one in the village knew the name of. When the men tried to kill it, it put up quite a fight: 23 of 66 got his hand chewed off, and several others were badly hurt.

"There's nothing like having more meat, but it does mean

more danger," our father said, and made 5 promise to be careful. 5 spent more time foraging in the forest or catching fish in the Lake than hunting. The men hunted in groups, but 5 liked to go about by himself.

"If something happens, you're on your own."

"I still prefer it that way," 5 said.

I felt very worried for him, and for 19 of 30 as well. 19 liked to be alone, just like 5.

"19, what do you think hate is?" I asked.

"I don't know. But maybe I have some idea."

That was a strange thing for 19 of 30 to say. To not know but to have an idea. What did it mean?

"You know before, when we talked about the first yesterday, a long, long time ago?"

I nodded.

"You said there were hundreds of thousands of people. I didn't know how to even think about how many that was," he said.

"Me neither."

"So, then," 19 of 30 said. "Instead of trying to think about it, you had to surrender to the number, like you gave your body to the water when you swam into the Lake. Then you'd have an idea of what hundreds of thousands feels like," he said.

"That's about all I know," he said, and laughed. "I don't think we're supposed to understand how many hundreds of thousands are or to feel what hate is."

I agreed with him. I liked thinking about things, but when I tried to think about things I couldn't sense with my body, they went cloudy, like when I wandered into the fog that sometimes settled around the Lake.

We sat there in the stillness for a while.

"Will you marry me, 8?" 19 said, quietly.

"Yes," I said, just as quiet.

I heard a rustling. Was it a bird? Or something a little bigger?

We took off our clothes. Lying in the grass on the shore, we had sex for the first time ever. I adored 19 and I wanted to be so close to him that I held on to his warm body as tightly as I could. There was the sound of stalks snapping, and something called out—*po po po po*. Perhaps the birds were raising a ruckus. A ripple passed over the surface of the Lake.

"Oh—"

19 of 30 let out a quiet sound. I closed my eyes and clung to him.

Something was watching us. I thought it might be the people who had died in all the yesterdays that had come before today.

"Oh—"

A sound escaped from me like a breath.

Slowly, the Lake was shrouded in mist.

\ The Drift \

I have been adrift for a long time.

I left home the year I turned twenty-five, which makes it more than thirty years now.

Traveling holds no joy for me. To tell the truth, I rather despise it.

"But it's your destiny."

The mother who raised me used to say this, as though it was some kind of curse.

I'd known since childhood that I would travel. Over the years, I was thoroughly inculcated with skills for life in the wild, for survival.

As the date of my departure neared, I tried pleading with the mother, but she didn't seem to hear.

"But I want to stay here with you."

"Destiny won't be moved."

As much as I resented her saying that as though it were nothing to her, it wasn't worth getting upset over. No—it was impossible, at least for me, to feel things for her like hate or love.

The day I was finally to leave, I cried just briefly. The mother did not. Instead, there as I watched, she stopped functioning. I could say that she died, but mothers are only mothers, after all, and there is no need to speak of them as if they were people.

The mother in the neighboring wing, who was raising a me that was ten years younger than I, told me that my mother had truly been saddened by our separation.

"There aren't many of us that can feel so much grief."

And yet none of it had ever been visible to me.

I left. The mother's sudden loss of function had surprised and distressed me, but I also harbored a sense of satisfaction— that if I had no choice but to live by the destiny I'd been saddled with, then she had paid the price for having raised me hostage to it, by letting it determine her own.

I am always alone when I travel. The exception being, of course, when I stop to stay in villages or towns where people live; but those are only brief pauses in my journey.

I have traversed wild plains, great rivers, deep forests, and at times come within sight of glaciers.

Aren't you afraid, traveling in such remote places? people sometimes ask.

I shake my head deliberately. Of course, I have experienced terror often—at night under my tarp, surrounded by four-legged animals with vicious teeth, or in the jungle, narrowly escaping being suffocated by a giant snake, or at sensing my body temperature plummet after mistakenly ingesting some poisonous plant. But those are foreseeable hazards that come with being away from civilization.

What I really fear is people.

After weeks of traveling without seeing a single other soul, nearing a human settlement causes something in me to draw taut.

After buffeting me hard but steadily throughout my time in the wilds, the wind takes on many smells and sounds around a town, almost as if humans have woven something impure into it.

It takes me many days from the time I first sense the presence of a settlement until I can enter it. To acclimate myself to the heat of the invisible storm formed of the complicated thoughts of its residents.

I stay with the watchers in each town or settlement.

The planet comprised many communities, from the smallest settlement of a few dozen humans, to the largest towns, with populations of tens of thousands. Watchers were stationed at each one: sometimes one, sometimes more.

My most recent stop was at a town in the northeast of the continent. The town watchers were clones of two men who were said to have designed the system currently running the planet—or so they claimed. Whether or not this is true, no one knows.

The communities were varied, and there was no overt communication between them at all. Each one already had its own history, a past, a culture. Over the thirty years I'd been on the road, I'd seen firsthand just how dramatically they differed. From subtle variations to major differences of values, if I started listing them I'd never reach the end. It really makes me wonder that these humans should be so various. It's commonplace for what is correct in one community to have precisely the opposite significance in another. There are some that attack without warning to drive me out as soon as I approach, while others greet me with astonishing curiosity.

The two watchers in the northeastern town, Jakob and Ian, were pleasant company. They led a quiet, modest life, Jakob being the yang to Ian's yin. They made a good team. The two of them begged me for tales of my travels. During my stay with them, we would sit in front of the fireplace every night and talk. Jakob made good coffee, and I'd tell them tales from my travels for as long as it took to have two cups of it. When the last sip was done, I'd wrap up for the night and retire to my room.

"So how's old Earth getting on?" Jakob asked, jovially.

He liked to say, *Humans have been trying to kill Earth for years.*

I didn't immediately know what to tell him.

Fundamentally, the planet was an accidental composite of discrete physical phenomena. It wasn't a unified entity that could offhandedly be identified by a name like *old Earth*. Having seen so much of it, I found it impossible to hold any one coherent image of the planet as a whole.

Someone who knew only, say, landscapes described in writing, or the sparkle of mountains and streams relayed through hearsay, or views seen on a computer screen, might easily fossilize such scenes in their minds and from there abstract the accumulation of innumerable such secondhand fragments into this idea called Earth.

But for me—knowing what I knew—such an act was almost impossible. Each of the places I had encountered was simply itself. They were all different, and always changing. Any attempt to fix and integrate them into "Earth" only yielded a terrible confusion.

If I could burst out into space and take in the entirety of this planet—perhaps then I would be able to believe in the idea of Earth. But the knowledge of how to enter space has been lost. Even the ability to fly the stratosphere is now only a matter of historical record. It would not be out of the question to create and maintain new flying machines for those who travel as I do, but flying machines didn't suit my nature. I preferred things I could guide with my own hands; the idea of relying on something while being ignorant of so much of its workings made me feel quite uneasy. So I traveled by hovercraft like the regular watchers.

"Earth? It's doing well," I said, circumspectly.

There was no benefit in being more precise here. I had to

allow myself the pleasure of ambiguity when I was among others, making conversation, at least.

"And what about humanity?" Jakob asked.

"Oh, they're much the different," I said, staying non-committal.

I couldn't imagine Jakob and Ian expected me to say more. It was, after all, an unspoken rule to avoid knowing about other communities.

"How about another cup of coffee?" Jakob said.

I'd had only one cup of coffee that night, but I declined. I didn't mind talking about my travels, but when I tried to think about the world as a whole, I was seized by an infinite tiredness that I preferred to hide from the two of them.

Could it really be true that they were the ones that had created the system governing humans worldwide today? If so, their optimism made me want to sigh.

Human evolution?

Such a thing could never happen under this system.

"See you in the morning," Ian said solicitously.

They went, Jakob pushing Ian's chair. The fire in the grate was just dying down.

I thought of watchers like me—and unlike Jakob and Ian, who were settled—as rovers.

My work was to look for new human communities that were outside the prevailing system. To that end, I roamed to all the corners of the world; as a matter of fact, however, there had been no such discoveries in all the time that the system had been in place.

I didn't like traveling and was deeply pessimistic about the future of humanity as it existed within the system. But I was intrigued by the possibility of encountering undiscovered communities. What would they look like? How developed were they intellectually, compared with us? There was ample possibility that they would have the potential for new genetic mutations beyond those we conventional humans could conceive.

Of course, it was highly likely that no such communities existed to be discovered. But I had hope.

"Aren't you afraid?"

I recalled what Ian said to me on the day I left the city in the northeast.

"Afraid? What of?"

"An undiscovered group could be . . . alien to those of us within the system."

"That's what I'm counting on," I said, cheerfully.

"And if they're unlike you . . . will you be able to live with that?" Ian asked quietly.

"I certainly intend to."

Ian frowned at me. He rested his gaze on me for several moments, as though he was sizing me up, and then looked away. Briefly, I felt something enter my mind. There was a flash of unfamiliar thoughts and images, and then it left.

"What did you find?" I asked, looking at him.

He had synced with me momentarily. I didn't care. Although

I objected to his ransacking my mind without so much as a by-your-leave, I had nothing to hide.

"Go well," he said.

I shrugged and smiled at him.

Around half a year has passed since my stay with Jakob and Ian in that large town in the northeast. I have been traveling alone again since then.

Even after thirty years, there are lands I have still not stepped foot in. And it is their untroddenness itself that gives me hope.

While I have not yet discovered a new community, just once, a quarter of a century ago, I came across a man in the wild, far removed from the nearest town or settlement.

I found the man wandering the plains, weak and emaciated. I approached him with caution. I wanted to prevent an attack, and if possible to avoid the need to attack him. If he was a member of an undiscovered human colony, it was essential that I capture him alive.

But when he opened his mouth, he spoke words I could easily understand.

"I'm not going back," he shouted.

I was crestfallen. If he spoke a known language, the chances of him being from a new colony were virtually nil.

"I'm never going back there again."

I had no choice but to deploy a sedative. Limp, his scrawny body was far heavier than I expected, and I had considerable trouble carrying him to my hovercraft.

I transported the man to the nearest settlement of mothers and left him there.

It became clear soon enough that the man was a normal human who was simply wandering the wilds after escaping from his town.

The mothers cared for him assiduously. His time in the wilderness had cost him most of the toes of one foot and two of his fingers, lost to frostbite.

There were several children in the settlement—children who would grow up to be watchers. They regarded the man with curiosity. The children were of different ages, the youngest still toddlers, the older ones nearly grown.

Although they were of different heights, the looks the children turned on the man were uniform. Whether due to his ignorance that they were genetically identical, or due to his weakened state, the man seemed to be oblivious to the strength of the affinity among them.

After some time, the man made a full recovery. He no longer spoke as much about not wanting to go back, but his attitude toward the children changed.

"I've seen you," he said, thrusting a finger toward one that was nearly fully grown. "You were a peddler at the edge of town."

The child nodded. Starting around age fifteen, the children were taught in detail about the towns and villages they would settle in as watchers.

"You were a lot older, though."

The man glared at the child. The child was unperturbed.

The man reached toward the child, and pressed the stumps of his first and forth fingers to the child's face, and cried out.

"This world's not right."

The child turned away, as though startled. A mother stepped between the two of them and pushed him away from the child.

After that, the man was kept away from the children. Later, he was returned to his town, whence he continued to attempt to escape. I understand he perished in the wilds.

The violence underlying the man's actions was uncomfortable; at the same time, I also felt some measure of sympathy for his motivations. Perhaps there was, paradoxically, something in common between his desire to get away and mine to stay.

Several years ago, I visited the town where he had lived. I went to his grave and scattered over it a handful of seeds I brought from the plains. If they survived, those pale blue flowers should be blooming right around this time of year.

I found them in the region just beyond the mountains.

No one had set foot in the region since a roving watcher several generations before me.

After navigating over the mountains, through the vast forest, and across the plains, I found myself amid smaller patches of woodland.

It was an odd place.

There was an almost complete dearth of larger mammals. I noted birds and insects, reptiles and amphibia, but the species differed significantly from those of other places, and the forms of many of them were unfamiliar to me.

I crossed the levels, traveled down a river that flowed through the woodlands, and eventually reached an area of dense growth, impassable by hovercraft.

The atmosphere was full of presence.

I bristled.

Something in me drew taut. There was a change in the air—smells, sounds, and lights all seemed different from before.

(Can there be a settlement here?)

I connected my computer to a storage battery and pulled the available geohistorical data. This area was a no-man's-land, unsettled by known humans.

Yet the presence persisted. It had the unique signature of a human community, distinct from that of other mammal groups.

I lingered for a week, trying to acclimatize to the unknown community's presence.

I was surrounded by thickets of trees, in which lived countless small birds. I hunted the species I recognized, braised them, and ate them. There was no river, but water was abundant—I had only to cup my hand against the moisture streaming over the rocks for it to fill immediately with water. The trees were also laden with fruit that was fresh and sweet.

Toward the end of the week, I started walking. The presence only grew thicker.

As I went on, the vegetation thinned out, and then I came onto open land.

Before me was a large lake with shores dotted by what looked like dwellings.

–

I saw creatures walking on two legs enter and exit the dwellings.

I thought instinctively that they were human.

Their stature was inferior, but in the formation of their limbs, and the development of their heads, they closely resembled us.

As I continued to observe them at closer quarters, however, I began to doubt my own instincts. For they lacked a nose, and instead were equipped with a third eye. Where the nose should have been were two gaping holes, presumably their external respiratory organ.

I maintained my silent observation for several days. They donned a form of clothing and also appeared to have some kind of language. I couldn't make out any meaning from it, but very occasionally I thought I caught a sound resembling a word from the universal standard.

Was it around then that I started to experience a subtle alienation from them?

My unease was not because they differed from us in appearance. Rather, some kind of preverbal, instinctive rejection dawned in me the more I observed them.

Although it disconcerted me, I seemed helpless to do anything about it.

I continued my observation despite this, trying to maintain as much composure as I could muster.

I hid my hovercraft in a stand of trees. Gathering only what I needed for my immediate survival, I cached it in packets distributed in the undergrowth. I constructed a basic shelter in the crook of the thick, strong boughs of a large tree trammeled by vines.

I hid among the trees during the day, waiting until sundown to creep close to the settlement. When night fell, I set foot in the settlement itself and peered into the dwellings.

I made careful notes on what I saw.

To my surprise, they had something like a written language. I couldn't discern a principle in the script, but I copied down the patterns that were carved at the entrance to each dwelling. On comparing them later, I noted the existence of undeniable patterns.

Their speech, too, seemed to have complex yet consistent rules.

(Can they be human after all?)

Repeatedly, I put off making a judgment, and hesitated, and changed my mind. All the while, my feeling of alienation from them mounted.

The creatures were exceedingly unhygienic. Aside from swimming in the lake that was the center of their settlement, they seemed to have no habit of bathing. Nor did they have a designated place for defecation, doing this when and where they pleased. Curiously, however, their excretions had very little odor. I attributed this to the potential presence of intestinal bacteria that broke down any offensive compounds.

I made a decision to focus my observation more closely on a particular bonded pair consisting of a young male and a young female. The pair often visited the shore of the lake to communicate, make physical contact, and occasionally undertake sex-like activity.

Soon I was able to get closer and closer to them. The mothers had trained me well in how to cloak my own presence.

During this time, I often found myself beset by tumults of primitive thoughts. What I characterize as a storm of thoughts has no physical manifestation, of course, but the creatures constantly gave off a stronger, coarser version of that same sense of presence that I sensed near a human settlement.

The pair's sex-like activity increased in frequency over the days in which I conducted my observation. The grassy bank of the lake evidently made a fine pallet for amorous ministrations.

Their sex filled me with an indescribable disgust. I was no prude. I made sure to sleep with women when the opportunity presented itself while I stayed in towns and settlements. Nor was I unacquainted with the copulation of other living things. In fact, I sometimes found consolation in the lovemaking of various life-forms as I went about my travels.

But not so theirs.

Persevering, I made myself watch over it.

The female cried out.

Soon, so did the male.

Their eerie noises made me want to cover my ears. Forgetting for a moment that I was hiding, I shuddered. Small birds took flight. I hid myself again, hurriedly.

The two creatures continued, heedless of my presence.

–

The discomfort I felt toward the creatures of the lake only grew with the passing of time.

They were too close to human.

Too close to what they could never be.

I suspected, perhaps, that they were a form of regressed human, but to even consider the possibility felt like a dirty thought.

Yes. By this time, a definite hatred for them had coalesced in me. I made my observations in my notebook with a shaky hand. My sentences were fragmentary and insufficiently objective. The reason was clear: I had lost all intention of seeing them fairly.

Why did I have to hate them so much? I was blind to my own feelings.

This had to stop, I told myself.

I had an inkling that to remain by the lake in such a state would be courting disaster.

I ought to step back and go to report to the mothers about these creatures. Then I would either come back or arrange for another roving watcher to study the colony instead of me. This was the path of action I decided upon.

There was just one more task I needed to complete before I left:

To make an analysis of their genomic makeup using the portable sequencing apparatus that each rover carried.

–

In truth, I ought to have done it much earlier. But I hadn't been able—hadn't wished to. The mere notion of such creatures being related to us made me shudder. And so I had delayed, day by day, to tomorrow, and the next day.

Late that night, I went to the location on the shore of the lake where the pair made their trysts, and set up the sample collector. As the sun rose in the sky, the pair arrived and copulated several times.

They left before sundown, but I couldn't find it in myself to retrieve the sample. I had to force myself finally to go and retrieve their epithelial cells from the collector.

The following morning, the machine spat out the results of its analysis.

The creatures' genomic sequence was 99.8 percent identical to that of known humanity.

Overcome by the bile rising inside me, I spewed up the contents of my stomach.

My memory of what happened next is hazy.

No—I'm lying.

I knew exactly what I was about to do.

I lay on my front beside the lake. The creatures fished, swam, drank, and washed their newborns in its waters.

They depended on it entirely, and I intended to poison it.

I couldn't bear for them to exist. I didn't want to tell the mothers about them. I was terrified that they were better equipped to adapt to life on the planet as it now was than we were.

Had they not been so closely related to us, my fear would not have been so great.

I recalled something Ian had said.

And if they're unlike you . . . will you be able to live with that?

I had been convinced that I could. Indeed, if only they had been closely related and superior to us, surely I would have accepted them.

I had failed as a watcher. Watchers were not supposed to make significant decisions. Only to observe and make slight adjustments. That was the task of a watcher, my destiny.

My fingers settled on the lid of the vial. Quietly, I opened it and poured the poison into the lake.

I resumed my journey.

Restless, I climbed over mountains and crossed rivers, drifting ever farther.

I traveled for longer than any watcher had traveled before. Where I had previously stopped and stayed for weeks in the communities and towns I visited, I now paused but a day or two. I avoided people as much as I could. I was far more at peace sleeping in the wilds.

I shared my secret with no one. I destroyed my observational records and said nothing to the mothers. I avoided the direction of the lake where the creatures had lived and bore the nightmares that visited me during the night with gritted teeth.

How long did I go on this way? I could sense my time was nearly up.

"Why not rest now?" the mothers said. But I had no intention of settling anywhere. Hadn't they told me themselves I was fated to roam?

I've never been able to shake my memory of the way the eyes of the female of the pair looked at me as she lay dying.

She'd smiled at me.

Even as the poison overtook her she smiled and said something.

I don't know what exactly it was, but I think she must have said:

"Who are you?"

Even there, on the brink of death, her eyes had been bright with curiosity.

I'm convinced that had they survived, they would have been far better suited to life than us.

They simply loved life, and all that lived. And so I know that even if—contrary to my imaginings—they were destined to eventually disappear within the greater flow of evolution, they would have departed this world as the last descendants of human life on the planet not with an unsightly struggle, like us, but with grace.

But none of that will happen now.

A long time ago, as we were parting, Ian wished me godspeed.

In my nightmares, she always says to me:

"Go well, you humans."

/ *Testimony* /

You have questions? For me?

I don't know what I can tell you. What? About a normal day?

You're a funny one. I mean, a normal day's just a normal day. Nothing more to it.

Hm? Normal's different for each of us, you said? I guess that stands to reason. So you compare these different normals, and? So what? Of course they're gonna be different. It would be weird if they weren't.

Well, anyway. If you're so set on asking, I've got nothing to hide. I'll tell you about it. Whatever you like.

Hmm, where to start. Even a normal day's gotta start somewhere. But where? That's the question.

Eh? When I woke up? Wow, you want to go all the way
back to then? No problem. I mean, no problem, but it might
get a little long, I just wanna warn you.

I woke up around age three. Everything up to there's kind of
foggy. I mean, I was three years old. Well, two, to be precise.
Two years, ten months, and ten days. I woke up, in the true
sense of the word, on the one thousand and forty-fourth day
after I was born.

Before the one thousand and forty-fourth day, I went to
sleep at night, like a lot of people, so my ma says. But my
memory of that time's pretty vague, so I don't remember
what it felt like. If you wanna know what it's like to be asleep,
you should talk to someone else. They get up and go to sleep.
Get up again. And sleep again. There's a lot of folk doing that
cycle, every twenty-four hours or thereabouts, so you can go
ask them.

Oh, right. You're one of those twenty-four-hour types,
too. Then you don't need me to tell you what it's like to be
asleep. Gotcha, gotcha.

So after spending the first three years—correction: two
years, ten months, and ten days of my life sleeping and
waking on a twenty-four-hour sleep/wake cycle, I stopped
sleeping completely. Someone I know at the lab once told me
why. My brain naturally produces high levels of some sub-
stance, and I have these pathways in my cells that metabolize
something else, and that does something that then means . . .

I'm sorry, I'm not great with names. Or people's faces,

that kind of thing. If you want details, you should go visit the lab. Yeah, they'll tell you all about it.

Long story short, after the age of three, or rather two, ten, and ten, I stopped sleeping. I haven't slept since, so that start of the day you mentioned, when I woke up? That's when it would be.

Eh? Not that kind of day? It's a normal twenty-four-hour day you wanna hear about?

I mean, sure, but there won't be much to say.

Twenty-four hours ago, I came here and sat down on this bench we're sitting on right now. And I've been here ever since. The end.

What have I been doing while I've been here? Nothing. Just sitting.

Thoughts? Not really. I just sit and feel the bench under my butt, and sense the temperature changing on my skin, and from time to time I notice how the light hits or the wind's blowing.

That's pretty much it.

Doesn't it get uncomfortable sitting still for a whole twenty-four hours?

Nah. Twenty-four hours is nothing. Or maybe twenty-four hours is forever. I dunno, but either way it's just a figure of speech. Time feels different to each of us.

Well, what's twenty-four hours like for you? You can talk, too, you know. You don't have to be the one asking all the questions.

–

Huh, right. You get up in the morning and wash your face.
Rinse your mouth. Eat a little food if you have any. Then you
walk around and study the geography or the flora and fauna
of the surrounding area while gathering fruit. By the time
the sun gets high, you're hungry again, so you cook what you
found, or food you preserved earlier, and eat it.

So you need to eat pretty frequently, huh? Isn't that a has-
sle? Oh, you find eating pleasurable? I get that some people
feel that way, but I don't understand it myself.

I don't eat much food at all. I need to keep hydrated, but
solids? I find they're a little hard to digest. By hard, I don't
mean that I can't. I know it's just a habit. In my case, they're
a little atrophied, but I have a stomach and intestines and a
pancreas and a liver, all of them.

Most folk have stomachs and intestines, but a lot of us are
missing spleens or thymuses. I'm actually unusual among
folk I know in being close to standard physically. Admitted,
the definition of standard hasn't meant too much for a few
thousand years now, but still.

My friend at the lab keeps telling me eating feels good
to him. He can catabolize, but not anabolize, meaning he
needs to eat to survive, so you can kinda see how he naturally ended up having a lot of feelings about it.

Oh, my color? Well, of course I'm a little green compared
to you. You're not the anabolizing type, either. I can tell just
by looking at your skin. It's a nice brown. Nothing mixed
in. Although personally I think skin without a little green
seems a little vulnerable. That might just be an unconscious

preference based on my idea that a having a body that doesn't anabolize must be a lot of work.

But we were talking about you.

Oh, yeah. You eat some food around noon, and then what? You write reports, or walk around and observe some more, and then, huh, think about things.

What kind of things?

What it means to be alive. Okay. Sure. That's a topic worth thinking about. So what do you think it means?

What? You're not sure yet? Jeez. I thought you'd have the answer. But I see how it works. If you had an answer, you wouldn't need to think about it anymore. I guess I should've known.

Who, me?

The meaning of life—I've never really thought about it. I mean, I'm already alive. Isn't it more interesting to think about real things that being alive brings us, over whatever it might mean? Like why some folk including my friend at the lab find it pleasurable to eat.

You wanna talk about me again?

Like I said, there's nothing too interesting. I sat down on this bench twenty-four hours ago, where I still am. Twenty-four hours before that, I think I was in a tree.

Yeah. On a branch near the top of the tallest of those giant trees in the middle of the sector.

I was there for around five hundred hours, if I remember

correctly. How long is that, in twenty-four-hour units? Nearly a month? Oh, right. It's not that long. I usually stay in one place for at least three thousand hours.

It feels good. While my body takes in the light and synthesizes. And the stronger the light, the better it feels, so you can see why I'd want to get to the top of that huge tree, can't you?

I've been all kinds of places. I probably know most of the good spots in the sector. But when I say good, I guess I mostly mean the ones that get the best light.

Sometimes I wonder if that feeling I get when I'm taking in the light is how it feels to be asleep, but who knows.

Dreams?

I don't have dreams. I don't sleep, remember? But I often find I forget when or where I am, and my attention jumps. Is that what you call a dream? No, no, that can't be it.

What? A daydream. Yeah, I know that word. If it is, I must have had all the daydreams in the world. I feel like I'm always having daydreams about this planet, all the way since the beginning.

There are all different ones, from daydreams about the very start of things on Earth, before life started, to ones about when it was teeming with life.

When I'm in a daydream, oftentimes it's like I've turned into Earth itself. Of course I can't tell what it must be like to be a thing the size of a planet, but still. It's almost like I turn into a part of it, sending out these little tendrils into the earth, soaking up the way it feels.

Ha ha ha. No, there's no way I can actually tell what the

planet feels, is there? It must be some misguided egocentricity in my unconscious that makes me have dreams like these. But no one can prove there's no truth to them, either, I guess.

But if you're wondering, Earth, well, it's not thinking much. I'm sure of it. And I'm the one having these daydreams, so take it from me. To the planet, us life-forms aren't even specks of dust. But sometimes we irritate it a little.

If we irritate it? That's a good thing. It's a lot better than being nothing. But either way, we're only talking about my unconscious's projection of Earth, so you could say it's all made up anyway, in a way.

You're asking if there isn't a time when I move around, without staying in the same place?

Of course there is.

When it's time to breed, I travel to all kinds of places.

I'm pretty close to species standard, so I'm compatible with most Fs. You might think that'd mean I have plenty of options.

But it's not like that. For some reason, the Fs seem to prefer folks that are far from standard. And when Fs desire Ms who are far from standard, their children end up being even further from standard as a result. Then those children are desirable to Fs, too, which is how the folks here that are my kin have ended up being so diverse.

There aren't a lot of Fs that choose me to reproduce with, so I walk pretty far to find them.

It doesn't feel great needing to look so hard, but walking's actually not too bad. I don't usually move around that much, so it feels different.

When I find an F, that's a relief. I feel lucky, and I'm grateful to them, you know? It's all about your attitude. Some folks say the functional stuff comes first, but I disagree.

When there's an F that meets me and decides they want to reproduce with me, I take real good care of them. After our reproductive period, if I bump into an F that I've reproduced with again, I'll always treat them to some water and have a little catch-up. We'll take in the light together, and lie there, and have a drink of water. It's nothing fancy, but it means the world to me. My Fs like it, too.

You wanna know how I reproduce?

Well, you don't hold back from asking the sensitive questions, do you? How about you, then? How do you do it?

It's just that, since there are so many different types of folks, that means there are even more different ways of doing it, right? Although I guess if you get down to it, what you're doing is basically getting your reproductive cells joined together.

But reproduction isn't just fusing cells, it feels good—you know, with that bliss, right? I know some folks don't have that, but for me, at least, I do. And so have the Fs I've reproduced with. Unless they were just acting like they did.

I often think I'd like to ask folks how they get their bliss.

You're going around talking to a lot of folks, aren't you? So tell me—how do they feel about it?

Huh. You're saying none of the ones you've talked to have said anything about it? Maybe it was because you didn't ask.

I hope you'll make sure to ask the next person you talk to a few questions about that.

I see, so you reproduce by bringing your and your partner's external sex organs into contact.

I'm really into that, too. But there aren't a lot of Fs that want to do it. It takes time, and trouble, and there's the risk that things can get awkward if you're not on the same wavelength.

That doesn't stop me from keeping on trying to find Fs that want to give it a try.

I like it when the F and I can hold each other. When I get my body up against theirs, and we can sense each other's breathing, it feels like finding something I lost a long time ago.

My ma left when I was five, but for the time we were together, she gave me plenty of affection. She'd always be around, looking at me lovingly and taking care of me in all these little ways, you know? We'd relax and take in the light together, side by side, her and me, and that felt good.

When I lie with an F, it brings me back to that memory of synthesizing with my ma.

Do you know there are even some folks in this sector who make families? Yeah, it's true. Not too many of them, I grant you.

Most of them are monogamous, but there are a few polygamous families, too. Their children stay living at home for a long time. Folk that grew up in a family—I don't know how to put it, but they're a little different from someone like me.

How? I don't know if I can tell you exactly, but let's see, maybe they're not as careless. I mean, you said so yourself—there are a lot of different normals. It's almost like folk that grew up in families, they don't have so many different normals. Kind of as if their normals are all the same.

The folk with families stick together. And they all defend each other. They make rules and punish those that cross them. And guess what—I was really surprised when I first learned this—in families, there are some folk that are important, and some folk that aren't. And the ones that aren't have to do as they're told by the ones that are.

Sounds like a pain, doesn't it? Having to do what someone else says? I wonder how that must feel. I guess it could be interesting, too, sometimes. Someone might think of something you wouldn't be able to think of yourself.

I did ask once if the folk that aren't important always stay that way. And then I was really surprised again, because I was told that if they overthrow the ones that *are* important, then *they* can be important instead.

Don't you think that sounds like a lot of work? Overthrowing people? That means, what, you gotta get them backed into a corner, right? I don't like getting into tight spots. I don't wanna have to go around backing anyone into any corners, either. All I'm after is to synthesize when I want to, and think about what I wanna think about when I want to, and do the things I wanna do when I want.

But the family-making folk seem to enjoy the way they do things. So I leave them alone. They can have their fun and leave me out of it. I've got no reason to go butting into their business.

I've got three kids.

Two of them anabolize, but one only catabolizes. The two that anabolize—oh, I called them kids, but they're both fully grown now. They'll just always be my kids to me, you know? I haven't seen them lately. They're both quiet folks, and I hear they've been at a spot at the edge of the sector for a long time now. They're probably really content there. Yeah, I get it.

The one who only catabolizes has some green in their skin, like me, but as far as I know they haven't done any synthesis yet. That one's still young and visits me once in a while. To run around and listen to the birds in the fields, and talk, that kind of thing.

Oh, and they like to eat me, too. Say I taste good. Yeah, they're always looking forward to eating, like some folk do.

Eh? Is it normal to let someone eat you?

You're really concerned about what's normal, aren't you.

Some do, some don't. It's personal choice. I don't do it much except with my kids, but I've sometimes done it with Fs I was reproducing with, mutually, if they were the synthesizing type.

Same as touching your skin together, eating and being eaten feels real nice. Personally, I don't do it unless it's someone I feel really comfortable with. But some folk aren't choosy and will do it with anyone. I know some people have views against that kind of thing, but I think it's all good. All it means is they need to synthesize again afterward.

I'll tell you something I heard, though. Just between us. Apparently, there are some folk out there who like to get others to eat up so much of them that they can't synthesize enough to make up for it. Isn't that something? I mean, keep doing that, and at some point there'll be nothing left of you. But if being eaten brings them bliss, then that's no place for anyone to be poking their nose in.

What do you think? You being the way you are about what's normal, I'd love to know what you make of these folk who go down this path where they get eaten so much they eventually disappear.

What?

You don't know, because you've never been eaten?

Well, sure, I guess you're right. If you're saying we can never really know what goes on for other people. Which is why I've been thinking all along there isn't any point you asking me all these questions. Hm? You still want to know?

Ha ha ha. That curiosity of yours is pretty interesting to me, too. There are a lot of different folk in this sector, but not so many of them have so many questions.

We're just all pretty different. Faces, skin tone, build, everything. Ability, too. Some folk can read minds, some start fires, some move air, some heal sickness. Some folk do nothing special. But whether that means they can't do anything, who can say?

Huh? You don't quite understand? No, I don't either, and I'm the one talking. That's just what I think.

So, we were talking about a normal day. My day.

Yeah, now that I try to talk about it, I don't get up to much. I'm just here. Sometimes I reproduce. And the rest of the time, I just am.

But enough about me. I'd like to hear more about you. Yeah, that's right. Could be some of your curiosity's rubbing off on me. Ha ha.

Watcher?

Never heard the word.

Huh. Different communities, you say. Across the world. With people. And children. Lived together every day. Plowing. Harvesting. Generally stable. Occasional conflict.

Conflict? What's that? Like when the family folk overthrow someone important so they can be important next?

Wait, did you just say that people sometimes die in conflicts?

Why do they die? They aren't sick? Or old? Or choosing to die?

I don't get it. If you die, you can't get eaten anymore, or eat anymore. You can't reproduce, or touch, or take in the light.

Sounds boring to me.

They get killed but they don't wanna die? What do you mean? They're forced to die even when they don't want to? Does that happen a lot? I don't believe it. That's ludicrous.

Okay, so it doesn't happen too frequently. Something like the folk who want to get eaten?

Not really, huh. They're healthy, and don't wanna be eaten, but death suddenly happens.

Yeah, this sector sometimes gets folk who arrive from outside. Usually not folk who are my kin—they're folk who are anomalous where they come from and were super isolated because of that. But once they're here they blend in and soon start mixing with us. My friend knows a lot about them, so go talk to them at the lab if you wanna know more.

Maybe those outside folk know about conflict, huh? No, I've never talked to any of them, or had the chance to reproduce with any that are Fs, so I don't really know.

But I can kind of tell. When I'm taking in the light, and having a daydream about Earth, I can sense that these outside folk have fears that we don't understand.

Do their fears lead to conflict? Dunno. But maybe they're a part of it.

True. I can read people, just a little. No, it's not like I know exactly what you've been thinking while you're sitting here with me. How it works is . . . I pick up hints of what someone's feeling. It just kind of flows into me.

But I don't know who these people are. Where they are, or what they look like.

It's gotta be—whoever it is, they want someone to listen. To what they're thinking. When people have something to say that's not being heard, they call out toward something they don't know. That's what I think. That's what I pick up. While I'm taking in the light, or being wetted by the dew, or blowing in the wind.

–

So you call yourself a watcher. Is there something you watch? Humanity? Hmmm.

Sounds like a big job. No, no, I'm sorry I laughed.

I mean, like I was saying earlier, to the planet, humanity's not even dust. So you're the one watching over something that's less than dust.

Do you enjoy watching?

I see. It's not about whether it's enjoyable or not. You watch because it's your job.

Why don't you quit?

You can't? It's destiny? No, it's more than that, it's the reason you exist?

I don't really follow. What you're saying all feels new to me. Truly.

Okay, there used to be a lot more of humanity. Mm-hmm, I see. But they went into a decline.

So what was the problem with that?

Mm-hmm.

Huh.

Wow.

But what was the problem with that?

You're a little nosey, aren't you. That's my impression. From what you're saying.

Why don't you stick to thinking about yourself some? The things you enjoy.

No? It's not that simple?

Okay, I mean, for me, it is pretty simple. The world, or

humanity or whatever, just means all of us, right? Me, and
me, and me, and you, and you, and you. If you wanna concern yourself with humanity, you can start with being concerned about yourself. If that's not enough for you, let's see,
you can think about the people you know—that's fine, too.

So then, if you and the folks you know are doing well and
having fun, that's gotta be enough. You can't get around to
doing more than that, and if you get it in your head that you
can, maybe you're overreaching a little.

Hmm, all right. All right.

I can see what you're saying. That we gotta look at the
bigger picture.

I know that in my head. But I don't believe in anything
aside from what my body knows. So I'm sorry, but what you're
saying seems like . . . a beautiful insect, floating in the air.

No, no, I'm not saying you're wrong at all. These floating
insects are beautiful. You should go see them. There are lots
that live in the woods that way.

Oh dear, don't get all het up like that. Wait, are you hungry? I remember that friend I mentioned from the lab told
me he can get a little het up when he's hungry.

Tell you what, do you wanna have a little of me? I taste
good—I promise, I'm good.

What a shame. He's gone.

Some folks are just impatient.

But it's interesting having these outside folk. This place is always changing, but even change stops being change when you get used to it.

I wonder how long I've been around, in twenty-four-hour cycles. Let's see—one, and two, and three, and four, and . . . . Huh, it's been something like three hundred years.

I haven't gotten bored of being alive yet, but if I get there, I don't mind dying. But the thought of being made to die, by conflict or something, like he was saying? No way. Count me out.

Oh, you came back. Yeah. You wanna try it?

We haven't reproduced, and you're not my kid, but I'll make an exception.

There.

What are you doing? Just eat it. What, you need to cook it first?

Huh. There you go, then. I lit you a fire.

Yeah, I can light a little fire, too. I forgot to say. That's right. Yeah, I can actually read you pretty well right now. I can read you, but I can still only understand what I can understand. That being the case I figure there's no need to mention it.

I think you're a little unhappy, to be honest, aren't you? I try to stay away from unhappy people. But there was something about you that interested me.

What? You like it?

That's great. But you're lying, I can tell. You're about to retch. Don't hold back. You can bring it up. I won't take it the wrong way.

Gone again. Too bad.

Yeah, these outside folk really are interesting. So he said there used to be a lot more people around. And that we can't go on this way. That something needs to be done.

I'm not so sure about that. What's wrong with the way things are? The number of people in this sector's been going down little by little, but it's not like that's caused any problems. You can't predict the future. And even if you did, you'd most likely be wrong.

Oh, you again. It was good? You aren't even lying this time. You used more fire, and salt, and you liked it that way, huh?

Okay, you're going now. Yeah, I enjoyed it. See you around. Tell me more about you sometime. I'm gonna go and be at the top of that giant tree for a while. Why don't we meet up again in another hundred or two hundred years? You take care until then.

\ The Miracle Worker \

The council was scheduled to start that afternoon, but because we were low on numbers, we decided to postpone until the following day.

"Could it be the weather?" White said.

"It's been nothing but rain lately, so perhaps."

"Why would rain be a problem?" White said, sounding amused.

"There might be watchers who need solar power."

"Hovercraft? I didn't know anyone still used them," White said with a shrug.

"I do sometimes," I said, and White shrugged again.

"You're funny, Maria."

It varied from region to region, I'd been told, but in the

past, most watchers used to travel by hovercraft. These days, most of us flew on compact hydrocarbon-fueled vehicles. I liked hovercraft, though—how ponderous they were. And to be honest, it scared me a little to get too high up.

"How many years has it been since the last one?" White muttered.

I counted on my fingers: *five years.*

Although I was hardly in the habit of keeping track of time, I knew that the last time the council had met, Aisha was ten years old.

She'd turned fifteen last week.

Aisha was a girl who lived in my sector.

I'd known her since she was born. Or, more accurately, since even before that.

Aisha's mother, Munira, was terribly poor. Munira had been orphaned as a young child and had made her own way ever since. She hadn't attended school, so she always struggled to find work that paid enough.

When the inequality in our sectors became too pronounced, watchers were allowed to intervene in a limited way. It used to be strictly prohibited, but now we were allowed to make adjustments in our own sectors if we could gain approval from the council.

But the number of those living in poverty in my sector was small, and there were no signs of their existence setting off any rapid or unnatural changes in the world, so I had no intention of getting involved.

I simply maintained a close watch over the poor of my sector. I felt sorry for them, but I wasn't in a position to care for them individually—that would introduce an imbalance in the equilibrium of the community. This was why I surprised myself when it came to doing what I did with Munira.

For whatever reason, I was drawn to her.

She had intelligent-looking eyes. Her voice was limpid, and her language, though basic, was full of warmth. The hard life she'd led didn't stop her from looking like she enjoyed every moment of it.

I met Munira at the bar.

I like my drink. I hear this is unusual among watchers. Those who become watchers are typically square, tedious, inflexible. Take the discussions at our meetings—most watchers insist on arguing from general principles, rarely if ever daring to express their own opinions. In fact, they'd rather not have opinions of their own at all, if they could help it. Among us, Jakob and Ian were the only ones I could imagine daring to say anything that might suggest they had any new ideas.

As a case in point, that so many watchers—most, in fact—don't even have their own name is already indicative of the issue. They said it presented a real problem at the time of the first council. I could understand why they decided on using characteristics such as size or body or hair color to refer to one another, but how must it feel to be called "White" or "Big"? If it were me, I couldn't stand to have such an insipid name.

Anyway, watchers are a boring bunch, but that's been true for millennia, so I don't need to keep harping on about it. I was going to tell you about the bars.

My sector has some wonderful bars. They have good snacks and a wide variety of alcohol. The inhabitants of my sector are greedy when it comes to pleasure. They're constantly improving their animal husbandry and breeding new varieties of crops to come up with increasingly delectable foods. They love music, and every night an array of performances takes place in spaces all around the town. The crowds don't just listen—they dance and sing along and have a good time.

The bars are no exception. There's always a band playing music to suit the mood, which, combined with the voices of the patrons, fills the whole place with a comfortable ambience.

Munira worked at my favorite of them all.

My first impression of her was that she was skinny. She looked like a teenager, but when I asked, she said she was twenty-three. After I'd seen her there a few times, we started talking. When I invited her to lunch on her day off, she was happy to join me and just as happy to let me pay.

Over time, she told me more about her life. She'd had a pretty difficult childhood, but she never dwelled on it.

I didn't see Munira for a while, so I asked the owner of the bar how she was doing.

"She's about to have a baby," he said.

For a second I was surprised, but then it all fell into place: the way her legs had been swelling as the evenings grew late, her dizzy spells, the loose clothing she'd taken to wearing.

"She was married?" I asked.

The owner shook his head.

"Nope. Won't say who the father is. Some deadbeat, no doubt. I'm guessing he up and left her anyway. Who'd do that to a girl like her?"

I got him to tell me where she lived and went to see her the next day. Her home, or what passed for it, was pretty shabby; in fact, it was barely standing.

It had pillars, just about, but what must once have been a kind of shack had mostly collapsed save for a single room. Its walls were full of gaps, and the ceiling was covered in tattered pieces of cloth that seemed to be intended to patch the holes in the roof.

"Hello," Munira said, sitting up. She sounded cheerful, but it seemed to take a lot out of her. "Come on in."

Most people would probably have been embarrassed by the humbleness of their home, but Munira didn't seem ashamed.

"Have you been eating?"

She was close enough to term that her bump was obvious, but her arms and legs were awfully thin, and her complexion was deathly pale.

"A little," she said, casually. But she quickly lay back down on her pallet again and closed her eyes.

After a while, I called her name. She didn't answer. I shook her shoulders, but she didn't open her eyes. She was out cold.

I rushed her to a doctor.

Munira ended up giving birth later that same day. She said she could only afford to stay in the hospital for two days, so on the third day, I brought her home with me. The baby was perfect. Munira said she'd decided on the name Aisha as soon as she found out she was pregnant.

"Even though you didn't know it would be a girl?" I said.

Smiling, Munira said, "Oh, I knew," and nodded.

Aisha was a healthy baby who explored and cried a lot, but at times when she needed to be quiet she would be docile, almost like she understood. Munira went back to work at the bar two months after she gave birth. I told her I could find her better work, but she refused.

"I like it there."

True, the owner treated her well, and the clientele wasn't so bad either. She said the owner had promised to feed her before her shift as well as after, and the bar was easy to get to from my house.

That's right. I'd made sure she didn't go back to the run-down shack she'd lived in before.

It was not long after she'd left the hospital, while she was still breastfeeding tiny Aisha, that I'd told her to stay.

She smiled and thanked me, and for the next few years we lived together the three of us.

–

When Aisha was three, she started predicting the future.

Late one sunny summer afternoon she'd said, "Big storm."

"*Storm*? Where did you learn a word like that?" I said, and told her to finish the rest of the meat I'd given her for supper. She never ate much. She wasn't picky, but I had the odd suspicion that she was reluctant to eat things that had once been alive, whether plant or animal. The only thing she ever asked for was water.

"Ummi home," she shouted, almost fearfully.

"That's right, she'll be home later," I said.

Aisha, almost in tears now, said again, "Big storm, Ummi home." She hadn't touched her food.

It was a clear evening. From somewhere I could hear the sound of music. The hum from the boulevard reverberated distantly, nostalgically. Constellations winked overhead, and the occasional shooting star streaked across the sky.

"Look how beautiful it is," I said, gathering her up. A gust of wind came in through the window, lukewarm and heavy.

Aisha started to cry. She slipped out of my arms and ran toward the front door. She flung her fists against it, making it clear she wanted to go outside.

"Well then, why don't we take a little walk to Ummi's work?" I said, and got our things ready. I put my keys and a container of water for Aisha in a small bag and closed the windows. Outside, the wind had picked up, but the sky overhead was still full of stars, a sliver of moon as slender as an eyebrow hanging over them.

As soon as the bar came into view, Aisha started running. She opened the door purposefully and went straight inside.

"If it isn't young Aisha!" the bar owner said, taking her in his arms and lifting her into the air. She fussed, kicking her legs out.

"Aren't we friends anymore?" he said jovially, holding her tighter. Aisha kicked even harder.

When he finally put her down, she ran to the kitchen as fast as her legs would carry her, crying, "Ummi!"

After a moment, Munira came out with Aisha and started a whispered discussion with the owner.

As soon as they were done, the owner clapped his hands together once, emphatically.

Turning to his customers he said, "So sorry, we're closing early today. Your food and drinks are on the house—on the condition you all get straight home. There's a bad storm coming."

A murmur went around the room, but in the face of the owner's insistence the patrons began leaving and heading off in different directions. Once the bar was empty, the owner locked up carefully. He brought in the sign from outside and latched the shutters, which he normally left open.

I walked home with Aisha and Munira, feeling as if someone had pulled the wool over my eyes.

"But the weather's perfectly fine," I said as we stepped through the front door. Just as I went to open a window to let a breeze through, a huge roar ripped through the atmosphere.

The storm that night was the worst on record.

Many homes were destroyed, and many people lost their

lives. The toll among those who'd been caught in the open was especially high.

Later on, I asked Munira: "Why did you believe her?"

"That's who she is," she said, as if it were nothing out of the ordinary. "I've known it since she was in my belly."

At first, I simply thought Aisha was especially sensitive to changes in barometric pressure. But her predictions weren't all about the weather.

She foretold that a cat would go missing, that our neighbor Ali would get appendicitis, that the wheat harvest would be poor, when the river would flood. By the time she started school, her prophecies became more detailed. They were so accurate that I grew a little uneasy—so much so I started to doubt whether I should be keeping her so close to me.

Aisha stopped making predictions shortly after that.

I was relieved, but I knew I needed to talk to her.

"Why did you stop telling the future?"

"I used to be able to, and now I can't," she said.

She was lying—I could see that much. But I didn't question her further. I knew that Aisha herself was struggling to deal with her prophetic abilities.

I thought she seemed happier when she started attending school. It seemed only logical, since her days of sitting at home telling us who was going to die next, and how, had been replaced by days playing innocently with children her own age.

I didn't know then that Aisha was developing a power that was even more powerful than her prognostication.

—

Around a month after Aisha started school, a woman came
to visit us. She said she was the mother of one of Aisha's
classmates.

"I don't know how to repay you," she said, repeatedly
making the sign of thanks with her hands. She swung the
bag she was carrying on her back to the floor, where it landed
with a thud.

"Take this, please. It was our fattest sheep," she said,
pulling meat out of the bag. Her family had herds, she said.
The hunks of meat, neatly skinned and cut from the bone,
glistened.

"But why?" I asked, confused.

The woman explained that Aisha had healed her daughter's leg.

"Healed her!" I cried.

"Yes. My daughter had a bad leg from a fever she had
when she was two. Aisha healed it."

"What did she do!?"

"She touched it," the woman said.

"Touched it?" I said.

In the several years that followed, Aisha brought many
miracles to the lives of the people around her. She restored
the sight of an old blind woman, made a man who'd been
crippled in an accident walk again, changed the heart of
an incorrigible rogue, and set a drug addict free from her
dependency.

—

People came to my house wanting to see her.

Some offered money, others meat. Some brought grain; still others, cloth.

Of these, Munira accepted as little as she could. Soon she was so busy receiving Aisha's visitors that she stopped working at the bar. Then she rented a modest house very close to mine where the two of them lived together.

I'd already informed the mothers about Aisha, but they hadn't shown much interest. They say the mothers used to be part of a powerful network that kept abreast of what was happening in every sector in order to keep the world functioning smoothly, but over the last few hundred years they seemed to have become rather inactive. None of us knew the reason. Presumably there was one—one that could be understood only by the mothers themselves—but they'd made no moves to enlighten us.

From what I understand, it was right around the time that the mothers became less active that the watchers' council started up.

The last one, five years ago, took place not long after Aisha started to be known in the sector as the girl who caused miracles. I touched on her case briefly toward the end of the meeting, almost like an afterthought. No matter how lightly I tried to pass it off, though, her story couldn't avoid drawing the attention of the other watchers.

"Is she a mutant?" someone asked straight away.

Of course, I had already conducted a genomic analysis.

"There was insufficient deviation to constitute a spontaneous mutation," I answered.

"Has that been confirmed?"

"I also conducted an analysis on the girl's mother. The father is unknown, so no conclusions can be drawn, but I detected no changes that diverged significantly from the average individual."

The crowd bristled. Then how did she cause these so-called miracles? What about the precognition? Could there have been some kind of error? Wasn't it just a trick? What was the lab's opinion?

I felt the watchers' cold gazes directed toward me. The voices calling it a common hoax were the loudest. Of course, I didn't entirely believe in Aisha's predictions or miracles, either. I couldn't yet rule out the possibility that her predictions arose from a state of delirium brought on by some psychological affliction. The same went for her miracles, if the troubles of those she was said to have cured had had their root in mental rather than physical causes.

"I believe this is unlikely to be a hoax, but only further observation will determine its true nature," I said loud enough for all the watchers to hear. They looked unconvinced.

After the meeting was over, the watchers immediately traveled back to their respective sectors. Watchers didn't tend to be the type of people who wanted to go out for a drink, even when the council brought us all together in one place.

"Everyone seems to like their own patch," White said under his breath.

"Aren't you going back to your sector, too?"

"I have to be there all the time. I want to take some time out when I get the chance to leave."

I shrugged. I hadn't expected White to say something like that, so I wasn't sure what to say. I'd assumed he was rigid and conservative like the others.

White and I went to find Jakob and asked him whether there were any good bars around.

The council always met in Jakob and Ian's sector. After thinking about it, Jakob answered:

"Not really. Although I know one place that might work."

"Where is it? Can you take us there?"

"Just follow me."

The place Jakob led us to was at the edge of town.

"This looks very exclusive," White said.

Jakob smiled and opened the door to his and Ian's house. The smell of a good stew drifted out. From a cage above the fireplace, a mynah bird chirped, *Home sweet home.*

Jakob, Ian, White, and I got into our cups until late that night.

Aisha stayed in school while continuing to minister miracles to the people who came to see her. It was strange to put it this way, but her miracle working was already proving to be a steady source of income. Amounts of money and food that were more than adequate for her and Munira to live on piled up at the house. Aisha should have had no more need to keep attending the sector school, which served mainly as a vocational training facility.

"But I feel at home when I'm there," Aisha would say.

At school, it seemed, she no longer committed miracles.

She sat in class, and ate her lunch, and chatted about trivial things with the other girls.

"Are there any boys you like?" I asked her.

Aisha blushed.

"What's his name?"

"My classmate Tahir," she said in a small voice.

With a shock, I was reminded that she was still a child. That she should tell me the name of the boy she liked—so trustingly, so openly.

Aisha and Tahir started being seen walking together. It warmed one's heart to spot them ambling through the town, chatting contentedly hand in hand.

Evidently, though, the sight didn't necessarily bring a smile to those who hoped to be one of her miracles.

"Please, give us more of your time."

"We need you to listen to us after school."

"We are all waiting for you."

The people waiting for miracles begged. It was true that Aisha was spending less and less time on them. Promises to see them often went unfulfilled, and many people were left waiting.

It wasn't long after that that Tahir's home was set on fire one morning before daybreak. The fire was put out before it spread too far, but it was clear that it had been started intentionally. Tahir's family forbade him from seeing Aisha.

After that, Aisha wasn't herself.

"I'm sorry," I said, stroking her head. Aisha kept her eyes closed for as long as my skin stayed in contact with hers.

"Why did I have to be born this way," she murmured.

I couldn't find the words to comfort her with. "I'm sorry," I said again, and hugged her tight. "What did Munira say?"

"She doesn't say anything, because I'm the breadwinner now. I'm the one who has to take care of the household."

"But you're still a child. You shouldn't need to worry about that."

"It's okay." Aisha shook her head slowly. "I already knew." Climbing out of my arms, she said, "I knew, actually, that it wasn't going to work out with Tahir."

She wasn't even close to turning fifteen yet, but the look on her face was adult.

That was when Aisha changed.

Where she'd done miracles singly and in private before, she started going out on the streets and proclaiming her prophecies. She announced the fates of everyone in the sector. She dug into the lives of the dead and told endless stories about them. To those who approached her with reverence, she bestowed gifts of miracles. She was outspoken about the direction she saw the world heading in.

She no longer went to school and most days even stayed away from home. She visited her worshippers wherever she was asked, granting miracles as she went.

Aisha's name became known throughout the sector. Soon there was an influx of visitors from other sectors seeking to visit her.

Compared to before, when the majority of people spent their entire lives in the sector where they were born, there

was already some gradual inter-sector exchange, but this was
the first time that so many people had streamed into a specific sector. I started getting trace requests from other watchers for travelers from their sector almost daily.

This council had been called around the time that the
population in the sector had ballooned to nearly double what
it had been.

"We're still waiting on a lot more," White is muttering.

On the second day, when we'd agreed to start the meeting, there was still only about half of the watchers in attendance. We decided to go ahead anyway. At the other end of
the great table in the conference hall, Jakob and Ian leaned
against each other, looking intently at a computer screen.
The watcher chairing the meeting, Curly, rang a bell. Its clear
sound rang through the hush of the hall.

I presented again about Aisha. Compared with the last
council, though, the response from the watchers was muted.
Most of them looked vacant, with slumped shoulders. Some
of them had laid their heads on the table. Even once I wrapped
up with a note on the increase in the sector's population, no
one had anything to say.

I turned and looked around the room. The only ones who
met my eyes were Jakob and Ian, and White, who was right
near the front. Even Curly was staring at a point somewhere
above and to the side of me with an absent-minded expression, mouth hanging open.

"What's going on with you all?" I asked.

There was no response.

The council adjourned shortly thereafter. The watchers, with the exception of me and White, scuttled back to their own sectors.

"Could be another coming," Ian said with a tilt of his head.

"A coming?"

"Don't you know about gods, Maria?"

Of course I was familiar with the concept of faith. That each one has its own gods, and that disagreements among them could be a cause of conflict. But that was ancient history—long gone, like a faded story you'd find in a file or a record.

"So what happens if it is?"

"I suppose things start to organize into a religion."

"The mothers told me that gods are brought into existence by things that are beyond the ability of humans to handle," I said.

Ian nodded. "So this world's facing more things we don't know what to do with, is it?"

"What kind of things would those be?"

"Things that humanity is powerless to hold back, I suppose."

"Like death?" White said quietly.

"But haven't humans always died?"

At my words, Jakob and Ian smiled just a little.

That night, White and I stayed the night at Jakob and Ian's again. There was roast lamb, dressed vegetables, and wine. A mildly depressed mood held sway over the table. What had happened to the watchers? Only a handful of the ones who hadn't attended had even sent word.

"What are watchers for, anyway?" White asked.

"What a thing to ask—at this stage!"

"How do you feel about it, then? About being a watcher?"

"I don't really know. I was just born to it." White cast his gaze up to the ceiling and kept looking hard at it for some time.

"Is there something up there?" I eventually asked.

"No, I'm just amazed at myself for living all my life the way I was born."

Jakob and Ian were looking at each other. White finally looked away from the ceiling, then finished the wine.

"We grow up with many of us," White said, slurring a little. Too much to drink. "Older ones, and younger ones."

"Of course."

"And ones that never became watchers."

"Yes."

"Do you know what happens to them?"

"I haven't seen any of them since I left."

"They live with the mothers their entire lives, and then they die."

I tried to recall those of me that I used to live with before I came to the sector where I kept watch. I tried to remember the me that was the watcher in my sector before I was.

I wasn't that interested in the other mes; the reason being, I knew all about myself. Older or younger, I was still me.
"There was one me I liked. He was three years younger
and lived a little ways away. We used to meet and talk almost
every day. He cried when I left to become a watcher. I still
think how good it would be to see him," White said almost
shyly, and then blinked several times.

For some time, none of us spoke. Then White slumped
over onto the table and fell asleep.

Aisha turned twenty. In addition to performing miracles
within the sector, she also started traveling to other sectors.
One journey led on to the next, and time passed—two years,
then five years, then ten. Munira traveled with her at first,
but later she began to stay home, citing the throng of believers that grew to surround Aisha.

"She doesn't need a parent anymore," she said sadly.

Wherever Aisha went, she was met with rapturous wel-
comes. Even among the believers who followed her, a hier-
archy started to form. Those closest to her took care of her
needs and received her guidance, which they then relayed to
the other believers.

Temples to Aisha sprung up in many locations. There
were statues made in Aisha's image and books made of Aisha's teachings, allowing her followers to venerate her even in
her absence. This stimulated new economic activity around
Aisha: not just direct commerce involving the offerings

made to her and the trade in related goods and services, but a wider-ranging social expansion accompanying the increases in mobility, construction, and infrastructure, and changes in people's ways of living. The circulation of currency continued to complexify.

It had become commonplace for people to move from sector to sector. The contact between populations with different customs often caused strife. Jakob and Ian called several meetings, but each one was attended by fewer watchers than the last. More than half the watchers were now impossible to reach, and requests to the mothers to replace them were rarely granted.

That was when the rumor reached us about the birth of another great mother.

"Do you ever wonder what the great mother's like?" White asked.

"Not really."

"I'd like to meet her. Haven't there only been a few of them ever born?"

"That's what I've heard."

I thought back to the mothers—peaceable, energetic, kind. Whether they were telling me off, or praising me, the mothers were totally placid. Emotional fluctuations were foreign to them, and they were never moved by sentiment. As a matter of fact, I didn't like them. That wasn't to say they'd caused me any mental harm or psychological injury. I'd just never really warmed to them.

"Did you like the mothers, White?"

"Oh yes. I still do."

"Do you ever wish you could go back and see them?"

"Actually, I snuck back, not so long ago," White said, in a low tone.

White and I had been meeting up at least twice a month as of late. Our work as watchers had taken a back seat—not only for the other watchers, whom no one could get hold of, but for us, too.

"You went back?"

"Yes, to the mothers that raised me."

"And? What happened?"

White nodded once, ambiguously, and said, "Hmm," before falling silent.

"Let's get a drink," I said, and White followed me out without a word. The bar where Munira used to work was now run by the old owner's son.

"The usual," I said, and the son, who looked exactly like his father, appeared out of the kitchen, drying his hands on an apron wrapped around a barrel belly that was also just like his father's.

"How are you keeping?"

"Keeping? I thought I saw you last month."

"It used to be every other day. I'm sure you've been busy," he said, looking between me and White, and smirked.

"Good to meet you," White said, holding out a hand. The young owner grasped White's hand firmly and shook it.

After clinking our glasses lightly and nibbling at the

young master's homemade smoked meats, we drank in silence for a while. White looked a little distracted.

"Was there something different about the mothers?"

White nodded again. "Hmm."

"What did you find?"

White drained the rest of the drink the young master had poured us in one long gulp.

"Nothing."

"What?"

"The mothers, the colony I grew up in, the other mes—they were all gone."

I couldn't understand what White was saying. They were gone? Had they all died? Could there have been a deadly outbreak of some kind? But would a human pathogen have killed the mothers, too?

"Are you pulling my leg?"

"If only."

When he went back, White said, the home he grew up in was gone, and so was any trace of the homes of the other clones he'd grown up with. Plants had grown over the places they'd once been, and there was no sign of the mothers, either.

"They didn't just move somewhere?"

"I don't know."

"I'm sure that's what happened."

"But they never said anything to me."

"You said you'd kept in touch with the mothers."

"I still talk to them."

"Then how . . . ?"

He could still get routine replies using the communication

templates, White said. But it was no longer possible to have a conversation outside of them. Why had they all disappeared? If they'd moved somewhere, where had they gone? Was there really another great mother now? And if so, where had it been born? What was happening around the planet? None of these questions ever got an answer.

"What about you, Maria?"

I thought back over my communication with the mothers and realized with a quiet shock that since arriving in my sector, I'd never once spoken to the mothers outside of the communication templates. It had never even occurred to me to say anything that was outside the realm of routine reporting, to dialogue with them in a way that had shades of dark and light.

For me, there was Munira and Aisha, and all the others of the sector.

"I really don't think I'm cut out to be a watcher," I said.

White looked at me curiously.

It couldn't have been long after that evening that White started spending more than half the week with me.

"I get lonely on my own," White would say.

"But you were on your own for so long."

"I had the mothers, and being a watcher."

"Which you still are, aren't you?"

White smiled, but there was something bitter in it.

The independence of the sectors had been as good as dead for a long time now. Isolation was over, the watchers in each sector were mostly AWOL, and the mothers were also effectively out of reach.

"I'm still watching," White said, and I shrugged.

What were watchers for? When White had asked Jakob and Ian, all that time ago, they'd explained it to us honestly: the rise and fall of the old humanity, the plan that the first Jakob and Ian had come up with, the isolation that had continued all this time.

I could understand the logic. But the notion of humanity that Jakob and Ian kept bringing up was something that meant very little to me.

The people of my sector, with their love of music, wine, and their neighbors. I knew them well. The people of other sectors I could also picture, if only vaguely, with other body colors, other customs, other tastes, other beliefs. In their own way, they existed, they were real. But—

Humanity?

That was too abstract, too vast. As a concept, the subject of some thought experiment, it could be interesting. But should such a thing heave into being, what would we—or the mothers—do with it?

"I like things the way they are," I said, touching White's wrist. Quietly, White embraced me. I closed my eyes and felt our breathing.

"Another miracle worker has emerged," Jakob presented, matter-of-factly.

It had been ten years since the last council. Six of us were in attendance: Jakob, Ian, me, White, and two watchers I was meeting for the first time. They both had names: Rien and 8 of 15. Rien was female, 8 of 15 was male. Rien was a normal name, but I'd never encountered a name like 8 of 15 before.

"Is there a story behind your name?" I asked, but 8 of 15 shook his head.

"If there is, I don't know it. The mothers gave it to me. They told me it was a token, but neither I nor the other mes ever learned of what."

"Oh, the mothers said my name was a legacy, too," said Rien.

"But why did we never know about the two of you before this?" Jakob asked them.

"I didn't know about this council either. I've come far. I don't stay in one place," 8 of 15 said. His demeanor was reserved, but I didn't find him at all unpleasant.

"I came from far away, too. There are a lot of people here."

Isolation had gradually been dismantled in Jakob and Ian's sector, of course, as it had been in mine and in White's. The routes linking sectors had been improved, and people now moved and settled in new places routinely and easily. Settlements in the sectors grew into large towns, multiple towns connected to make cities, and there was constant interchange between them.

"It's so busy here, it turns my head around," Rien said, laughing.

"The mothers told me to come here," 8 of 15 said earnestly.

"Do you communicate with the mothers who raised you, outside of the templates?" Ian asked.

Rien and 8 of 15 both shook their heads.

"No, not these ten years or so. Their message about attending the council was sudden, and they didn't answer any of my questions," 8 of 15 said gravely.

The new worker of miracles was a man.

"What's his name?"

"Suuno."

"What kind of things does he do?"

"Very different ones from Aisha. He performs some miracles, but his main talent lies in being a teacher and leader."

"How large is his following?"

"It's growing by the day."

Suuno had been born very close to Jakob and Ian's house. Their sector had thrown up many children with anomalies, so they'd kept an eye on him, expecting him to be the next, but they hadn't found any mutations in his genome.

"What's more, we haven't had a good grasp of the children with mutations in some time now," Ian added quietly.

"I remember," he went on, "how back when the sectors were well isolated and their populations were in the thousands or tens of thousands, even when a leader appeared within a sector, their authority tended to be undefined."

Rien nodded in agreement. "It's still that way where I am. Some of the leaders are hunters or farmers, sometimes they're diviners who pass judgment on people, and other times they're more like representatives who don't do any of that at all."

"That's right—and up until just decades ago, this sector, Maria's sector, and White's sector were all like yours. But with the abolishing of inter-sector isolation, we've started to see clear demarcations between the metropolitan centers and the surrounding areas, alongside which the formerly amorphous influence of regional leaders has been formalized and entrenched, leading to the establishment of a burgeoning elite."

Ian looked around in turn at each of us gathered there.

"All that, and now religion," Jakob muttered.

"Yes, politics and religion. The center and the periphery. Traffic and hybridization. The same stages that the old humanity went through are being reproduced, albeit on a far more rudimentary, simplified scale."

"Do you think the situation has anything to do with the birth of the great mother?" I said.

Rien turned to me in surprise.

"Is the great mother really back?" she said, with a light in her eyes.

I paid Munira a visit for the first time in a while.

"Look at you, Maria. You don't change a bit," she said, steeping a pot of herbal tea. Her hair had gone snowy white, and she had a hunch now. The skin of her face and limbs was covered in fine wrinkles.

"I've been sick," she said, pointing to her abdomen. "Got a bad growth in here."

The tea was pungent.

"Aisha's powers couldn't touch it." Munira shook her head as if to say, *It is what it is.* Then she smiled slightly. "I don't mind. We all die sometime. But I hate thinking of how Aisha will feel."

"Is she upset?"

I'd heard a rumor that Aisha's teachings removed the fear of death.

"Well, when she's doing her miracles, she's bigger than life, but when it's her and me, she's just my little girl."

We sat across from each other and drank our tea, reminiscing about when Aisha was young. Then Munira told me about the trips that she had accompanied Aisha on: the desert roads that seemed to last forever; the bands of merchants they'd met; vast herds of camels; her first sight of the ocean. Dolphins that played in the bay; the crowds of people who waited for Aisha, and their rapture.

"Who was her father?"

I'd wondered for a long time and never dared to ask.

"No one."

"What?"

"I never had sex with anyone."

"That can't be true."

Munira smiled weakly again. *You don't have to believe it, but it's true. Aisha doesn't have a father.*

"She's like me," I said, before I could stop myself.

Startled, Munira looked closely at me.

"Really? But you don't work miracles, Maria."

"It's true. I don't have a father, or a mother, either."

Munira tilted her head as though to say, *I don't*

understand. Suddenly looking exhausted, she said, "I'm going to go lie down."

I took my leave and went, promising her I'd be back next week. But she died before I could keep that promise. Aisha was traveling, so I conducted the funeral along with people from the neighborhood. The old owner of the bar cried a lot. *My sister, my daughter,* he wailed, drawing her dead body to him, deep in lament.

Twenty-five more years passed, and in that time Aisha died, too, as did Suuno, the other miracle worker.

A leader in the elite had had both of them captured as criminals and beheaded. But their followings only grew. There were efforts to suppress them, but they survived. A new leader took the old one's place, and another, then another. The suppression changed its form, and eventually the sects formed by those who followed Aisha's and Suuno's teachings were permitted to practice openly.

"Money talks," Jakob explained simply.

Both groups now paid large sums to the central government, and any friction was long in the past. We were holding meetings yearly now. After Ian died, and White died, and 8 of 15 died, the council's members were down to Jakob, Rien, and me. Even after their deaths, we didn't get a new Ian, or a new White, or a new 8 of 15. We'd been gathering each year at Jakob's house as if to lean on one another, to hold one another up.

When White died, I was astounded at the depth of my

sadness. I'd believed I never loved White—just thought I'd found someone I didn't mind having beside me. But it seemed that things had gone beyond that. It took me a great deal of time to recover from the sense of loss.

"There are more humans now than ever," Rien says.

"They're growing exponentially."

"Have you heard from the mothers?"

I ask the question we ask every time we gather. It's twenty years since we've been able to communicate with the mothers. We tried returning to the places where we'd each grown up, many times, but all of them had been reclaimed by nature. The houses where we'd grown up, our other mes, the mothers—all gone.

"Do you think the great mother's out there somewhere?" Rien says fondly.

"You're still thinking about her, Rien?"

"I am. The mothers said that a me many, many generations back was raised by a great mother."

Jakob glances at the wheelchair in the corner of the room.

"That's Ian's chair, isn't it?"

"That's right. He used to like our walks."

"Don't you keep a bird anymore?"

"Not now that he's gone."

It won't be long before the three of us are gone, too. But does that mean we won't see what becomes of humanity after us?

"What were we, in the end?"

"Frankly, the first me and the first Ian—the ones who came up with the original system that made the world like this—didn't have a lot of faith in anyone. Not the watchers, not the humans."

"And now?"

"Not much has changed there."

"Why? There's more and more of humanity every year. Wasn't that you and Ian's goal?"

"There may be more, but they can't just keep going down the same paths."

"I don't know. It sounds complicated," Rien says.

We still call it a council, but now we simply gather to talk and have dinner together.

"What shall we eat tonight?" Rien asks Jakob.

"Let's grill some lamb and throw a salad together. I have a good wine I think you'll like, Maria."

Where have the mothers gone? The world we live in now feels almost like a dream to me these days. Am I the one dreaming this dream? Is it the mothers? Or even . . . ?

Sounds of worship arrive on the breeze. It's the Suunists' six o'clock prayer. Beats of drums large and small reach us quietly through the evening darkness.

The same paths, Jakob said. What was White doing now? Now that he was dead, was he gone forever? Or was he waiting, somewhere in a single cell, for the next time he would open his eyes?

"I hope we meet again," I murmured.

Rien, who was making the salad, turned around.

"We'll meet again, somewhere, someday," she said, as if in a dream.

/ Love /

When Kyla joined the lab, I felt an incredible sense of relief.

I could tell from the start: Kyla and I were the same kind of person.

Kyla came here five days after the rain started.

"You know, we often get newbies when it's raining," Em had said, and then Kyla arrived with her small rucksack that very afternoon.

Em asked her, "Did you get here on your own?" and she nodded. Em bombarded her with questions. Which village were you in? How long did it take to get here? Did you see any animals on the way? What are your abilities?

The mothers seemed to have been expecting her. They took her aside and saved her from Em's questioning, made her take off her wet clothes, and sent her to a hot bath. I was in the back of the room, watching her from a distance.

Kyla was shivering ever so slightly. Whether because she'd caught a chill from the rain, or she was afraid of something, or just in anticipation of something that was about to happen—I wanted to know, but of course there was no way I could have known anything at the time.

Kyla was assigned to the room directly above mine.

For the first month, Kyla didn't leave her room much. That was normal for new arrivals, so it didn't raise any red flags.

From time to time, I'd hear her footsteps. Quiet ones, that went *pth, pth*. Her footfalls were so light, you'd have missed them among the sound of the wind and people talking unless you were really listening. When I caught her footsteps, it was like I could picture all of her petite body.

After a while, in among the sound of her footsteps, I started to hear the sound of her door. Around dawn, Kyla would leave her room and go out somewhere. She usually came back around half an hour later. Then, for a while after that, there'd be more modest footsteps—*pth, pth, pth*.

Welcome back, I tell her in my heart. For a moment, her footsteps pause. Then they continue, *pth, pth*, just much more quietly than before.

—

Early one morning, after hearing Kyla's door, I left my room. Her footsteps were heading to the stairs. Without hesitation, I ran over to them and caught a glimpse of Kyla's feet coming down the steps.

"Good morning," I said to her, gently.

"Good morning," she replied, gently. Her eyes lit up. Warmth filled my chest. She remembered me.

We went down the stairs together. The assembly hall on the ground floor was dark. We walked side by side to the big window facing the river. I opened it. Damp air came in.

"It rains a lot here, doesn't it," Kyla said.

"Yeah. That's why the river keeps changing."

"What's that over there? The water's a funny shape." Kyla pointed to a spot off to the side of the main flow of the river, which made whorls like a giant snake. Giggling, she said, "It looks like a baby snake."

I got it. If the river was a big snake, then you could kind of see that part where the water pooled as a small snake it had given birth to.

"That's the Crescent Pool," I told her.

Kyla nodded and made a small humming noise.

Another gust of wind came through the window. Kyla smiled. "Noah, you're a scanner, aren't you?" she whispered.

"Yeah. You too, Kyla?"

"Me too," she said, looking happy, and kissed me on the cheek.

—

After the day we watched the river together, Kyla became more sociable.

At dawn, she'd leave her room and drink tea in the kitchen. I woke up as soon as I heard her moving. When I washed my face and went down to the kitchen, Kyla would have tea ready for me, too.

"I thought you'd be the kind of person who likes brown tea," she'd told me the first time, and since then, I really grew to like it. I used to prefer black tea, but the brown tea that Kyla made was actually really good.

After drinking her tea, Kyla rushed outside. I went with her sometimes, but most days she walked around by herself.

She always came back for breakfast. With tree leaves in her hair, or her clothes soaked.

With my eyes, I'd ask her:

(You must have been in the forest.)

(How cold was the Crescent Pool?)

Kyla would answer me with a nod or shake her head.

Kyla started taking classes, too. They were for people who wanted to receive a standard education.

"I went to school for a while, back where I was before," she told me.

"What's school really like?" Having grown up here, I knew how schools worked, but never having belonged to one, I'd always wondered.

"Oh, you'd know if you scanned me, wouldn't you?"

"No thanks. I'd rather avoid scanning people without their consent."

"Huh. I don't care what you find out."

"That's because you're a scanner, too."

She looked into my eyes.

"Then you don't mind if I find out, either, do you?"

I looked down. Truth be told, I didn't want Kyla to know everything I was thinking. For one thing, even I didn't know everything I was thinking. I didn't have a clue what kind of darkness could be hiding inside me.

"Don't worry, even I can't read your unconscious," she said, like it was nothing.

"Wait," I gasped. "Kyla, are you scanning me right now?"

"Yeah."

"But I don't feel anything."

"Really?" She was smiling.

"I should be able to feel myself rejecting the unwanted incursion," I said, taking a step back.

Kyla stopped smiling. "I'm sorry, I won't scan you anymore," she said, and took my hand. Tears welled up in her eyes and spilled over.

"I'm sorry, too. We should get to class," I said, pretending not to see. I wasn't great with girls when they cried. I never knew what to do. But I knew what I really wanted was to dry Kyla's tears for her. Then put my arms around her and kiss her softly.

Pale green thread slithered through and across the cloth. Right in front of my eyes, it became a grassland.

Kyla turned the cloth over, tied off the thread, and clipped it with scissors. Then she gathered several different colors of fine brown thread and threaded it through her needle. Her fingers moved swiftly over the cloth, and a forest appeared behind the prairie.

"You're so good at that," I said, and she nodded without looking up.

"My mom taught me."

"Your mom must have been a pretty good embroiderer."

"Yeah, my sisters are, too."

So she'd grown up with a family. There were no families at the lab, as a rule. They said that back when there'd been more people at the lab and in the surrounding colonies, many of the lab people had made families, but now that there were fewer people here, there were no more families at the lab. Those who wanted to form families usually left the lab and went to live in the colonies nearby. At a stretch, you could probably call the whole lab one big family, but that didn't seem quite right. The lab was the lab.

Some of the newbies who'd grown up elsewhere came from villages with high numbers of family units. But the mothers said that those who came here, even if they'd originally been born into families, had been ostracized by them from a very young age.

"Did you get along with your family, Kyla?"

"Yeah," she said, as if it was nothing special.

"Isn't that pretty unusual?"

"Why?"

"They say it's only people who don't fit in at their villages that come here. And that most of them have problems with their families, too."

"I didn't have problems *all* the time."

"Then why did you come here?"

Kyla went silent. I felt nervous that she might be about to start crying again. But she didn't.

"I wanted to see what was out there in the world. That's all," she said, gazing into my eyes. That made me feel even more nervous than when I thought she was going to cry. She went back to her embroidery. Her needle created a sun over the forest, and a colony of rabbits in the prairie grass.

Kyla had such a pure laugh.

Before I knew it, the sound of it started drawing people to her, so a crowd would gather whenever she was in good spirits.

"Everyone likes me," she said, in a singsong voice.

We were drinking tea together at sunrise. I was feeling a little jealous—at not being unable to keep her to myself.

"You should join us, Noah."

But I shook my head. I'd been born and raised here, but I didn't really fit in. I was always alone.

At the lab, some of us, like me, could scan the minds of others, while some could light fires out of thin air. Some people could move things without touching them, and some could predict the future. We all looked different, too. People with three eyes, people who walked on all fours. People who breathed through gills, people with divergent metabolic pathways. I'd heard that in the outside world, everyone could reproduce with anyone of the opposite sex, but here there were several people whose type meant they were only compatible with certain partners.

"Is it important to reproduce?" Kyla asked the mothers.

"It would seem, since you've been born with a body with the ability to reproduce, that you might find it fulfilling to use it."

At their response, Kyla looked a little quizzical.

"Don't mothers reproduce?"

"No. We have a different way of self-replicating."

"I see," Kyla said. "If I were to think I didn't want to have children, would that be a bad thing?"

"Of course not. But it would be a little bit of a waste."

"Why?"

"Because you're all very important."

Kyla opened her eyes wider. "We're really that important?"

"You are. Everyone here was the hope of humanity."

"Was? Aren't people here because they've been cast out of their villages? What's important about that?"

"I suppose it's because . . . humans are naturally resistant to taking in outliers."

"Why? We're all so different here, and we get along fine."

"It must be because for all of you, the things you see here don't register as being very significant differences."

When someone died without making children, a new clone of that individual would be generated. If that clone died without any children, then they'd be cloned again. I was a clone who'd been made from generations of clones of the first Noah. But the longer a clonal line got, the more risk it had of failing to differentiate into human embryos.

Kyla laughed and said, "That sounds complicated."

We had a lot of freedom at the lab.

Kyla and I lived in the main wing, supervised by the mothers, but others lived self-sufficiently—or nearly that way—in the surrounding forest, or by the river.

I'd always preferred to keep to myself, but sometimes there'd be people I could feel comfortable with, like I did with Kyla.

One day, I went to visit 30 of 1 and 2 of 6 at their home. They lived in a cabin with a thatch roof near the water.

"Wow, hi!" The twins, 4 of 1 and 5 of 1, greeted me at the door.

"Have you been well?" I asked, lifting 5 of 1 up into the air.

"Me too! Me too!" 4 of 1 shouted.

30 of 1 came to the door.

"Where's 2 of 6?"

"He's out fishing."

4 of 1 was trying to climb up my leg. "Ow, cut it out," I said, but 4 climbed higher, panting happily. Half pushing 5 aside, 4 nestled into my arms, too. 5 was hanging upside down by this point and in danger of escaping entirely.

"What's up? Something on your mind?" 30 of 1 said.

"Yeah," I mumbled, but it must have gotten drowned out by the twins' cries, because 30 was still waiting for me to reply.

I came out with it. "I've met someone I like."

30 smiled. "I'm happy for you."

30 made us some tea. It was always really muddy, and I could barely drink any of it, but 30 always gave me tea. Then she would say, "The tea—you don't need to drink it. It's just a sign of friendship," and gently wave her delicately webbed hand in my direction.

Two years after Kyla had arrived at the lab, the distance between us still hadn't closed. In spite of that, we kept up our tradition of having tea together at dawn.

"I'm a little bored of this place," Kyla said, drinking brown tea. "Why are you here, Noah?"

I was kind of taken aback. I'd never thought about it. Why was I here?

"Don't you ever feel like leaving and seeing what's outside the lab?"

While I was thinking about her question, Kyla left the room.

Because Kyla was an early riser, many of the lab's residents had taken to waking up early and joining her when she went to walk in the forest or swim in the river. I was always worried that she would find a special someone to love. Getting her seemed like a hopeless task.

Yes, I'd thought about scanning her mind. But scanning rarely gave you good answers. People's minds were pretty chaotic. Even if I could get in, dig up any lost memories, and reconstruct them all, I was sure the result would be too complex and layered to crystallize and extract easily. To be fair, though, I'd never tried running the ultimate scan—never been all the way down to the deepest part of anyone's mind.

Could that have something to do with why I myself didn't know why I was still here?

I kept thinking about what Kyla had said for days afterward. The answer always seemed just out of reach, but in the end I didn't find it.

Instead of giving Kyla an answer, I went back to her with another question.

"What is it about this place that bores you?"

She laughed—in her pure, clear voice. "Everyone looks so happy here."

Kyla's embroidery was on display all around the lab. When I looked at them, I got a weird feeling. Each piece was of a familiar landscape from somewhere nearby. The wind was blowing across the swaying grass, and water was flowing. It was just needlework, but they made me feel as if the forest was there, and the river was real.

"More rain," Kyla said, glumly.

It had been raining for ten days now. In the kitchen, there was the smell of something rotting. I'd gone to the forest earlier that day and dug a big hole to bury the garbage in.

"Noah, you're soaked," she said, touching my hair. I jumped. I noticed the herbal scent she wore. A sweet, clear smell. A smell that reminded me of her laugh.

I hugged her. I don't know what gave me the courage. Kyla held still, and so did I.

"Aren't you going to kiss me?" she whispered.

Kyla's lips were softer than I'd imagined. Her small tongue slipped into my mouth. I let mine wrap around it. It was so warm inside our mouths. I wanted her badly.

"Let's make a baby," she said, and hugged me back.

Kyla and I left the lab. We built a small cabin with a thatch roof right by the river.

"Are you sure?" the mothers asked me.

"Of course."

"You can come back anytime, Noah," they said. I wondered why they were telling me that. But the excitement of being able to live alone with Kyla won out.

"What about me?" Kyla said. The mothers stayed silent. Kyla laughed. What a beautiful laugh, I thought, but at the same time, I felt a little weird about it, too.

"We hope you'll be happy together," the mothers said, waving at Kyla and me as we left.

Kyla giggled and whispered just to me. "We're already happy, aren't we?"

We moved into the cabin with the thatch roof, which made us neighbors with 30 of 1 and 2 of 6.

Kyla didn't feel comfortable with them at first.

"They just look so different from us."

"They look a little different, but 30 and 2 and their twins—they're all human."

Kyla nodded.

"They're human, even though they have three eyes and no nose?"

"Those are pretty minor differences, actually."

I knew that the village that 30 of 1's and 2 of 6's ancestors were from had been wiped out through the actions of one man. The last surviving inhabitants had been brought here after the mothers rescued them on the verge of death. That was more than a thousand years ago. Although their descendants were able to reproduce with most of the types here, they tended to keep to themselves and still rarely mixed with people who were originally from here.

To my surprise, though, Kyla soon became close with 30, 2, and the twins.

"They're wonderful people," she'd say, and go over to their place practically every day. Kyla taught them needlework, and 30 of 1 taught us about the different plants that grew in the forest. 2 of 6 taught me how to fish, and I taught him how to cook with herbs.

It was the rainy season when Kyla fell pregnant.

"The river's looking different again," she said. She was in bed with morning sickness.

"How can you tell?"

"I'm running a scan on 2."

"Is he around?"

"No, he's pretty far away. Other side of the river."

I hadn't known that Kyla could scan people from such a distance. I definitely couldn't.

"You shouldn't scan people without their consent," I said,

sullenly. I was feeling irritated, a little more than usual. I chalked it up to the never-ending rain.

"It's okay to feel frustrated," Kyla said, smiling. "I don't like when it rains too long, either."

It was as if she'd read my mind.

"Get out," I said, instinctively. I was surprised by my own words.

"I'm sorry."

"It's okay."

Kyla was understanding. My irritation stuck around for the rest of the day.

Inside love, there was hate.

That was totally new to me.

Life with Kyla was good, and our baby girl was adorable. It was Kyla who had named her Lala6.

"That's an unusual name."

"I've always liked names with numbers in them," she said, pleased.

I felt another surge of irritation. I regretted it immediately.

Kyla was great. She was cheerful, and hardworking, and kind. But for some reason, when I was with her, I felt trapped.

"That's just the price of being with one woman," 2 of 6 told me, but he was smiling.

I started going back to the lab sometimes. When I was with the mothers, I finally felt my equilibrium come back again. It wasn't that I'd fallen out of love with Kyla. I just felt suffocated for no reason.

–

Kyla got pregnant again.

"I hope it's a boy," she said.

"Me too."

Lala6 pulled herself up to standing using my leg. She burbled happily.

"Good girl," Kyla said, laughing. I realized it had been a while since I'd heard her laugh.

"Is the morning sickness giving you a hard time?"

"No, not at all."

Lala6 tripped. I bent down and picked her up. She fussed and writhed. When I put her down on the floor, she grabbed my leg again. I thought about the time 30 and 2's twins had climbed up my legs outside their cabin.

"You prefer 2 of 6 and 30 of 1's children over your own," Kyla said. She sounded utterly calm.

I couldn't respond, because she was right.

"It's okay," she said in the sweetest voice.

Our second child was another girl. Kyla named her Mimi2.

Lala6 and Mimi2 were healthy kids. Our home was once again filled with Kyla's laugh. But it was never directed at me. Kyla was head over heels for Lala6 and Mimi2. It didn't seem to bother her in the slightest that I spent almost all my time either at the lab or at 30 and 2's cabin.

"Don't sulk. Of course a mother is going to be devoted to her children," 30 would say, but the reason I didn't want to be around Kyla wasn't because she was too absorbed with the children to pay attention to me.

No—something was wrong. Something.

Maybe I already knew the reason I was feeling this way. I just didn't want to face it.

"Kyla scans people without telling them," I tried telling 2, in a whisper. "Did you know?"

"Are you sure?" 2 didn't seem to believe me, but I was sure. It wasn't just 2 of 6 and 30 of 1. I was convinced she had to be scanning me, too.

I talked to the mothers about it.

"Well," they said, expressionlessly.

"What should I do? What can I . . ."

The mothers didn't respond.

I went back home. That night, as she lay asleep beside me, I decided to scan Kyla's consciousness, just for a minute. She didn't reject me—even though she should still have resisted the scan in her dreams.

I'd intended to get out of Kyla's mind right away. But I couldn't help stepping deeper and deeper into her.

Her heart was beautiful. She loved me. She forgave me for being suspicious of her. She loved me, and our children, and her old family, and the mothers, and the world. Her love was so pure. I was devastated.

The mothers took me away from Kyla.

"You're experiencing a minor breakdown," they said. I didn't resist.

Kyla comes to visit every week. She comes into the room at the lab where I'm staying with the mothers. She never comes in alone.

"When you get a little better, I'll bring the children," she says, sounding loving. I nod weakly.

The mothers bustle her out of the room, take her away from me. Neither of us puts up a fight.

When I ask the mothers, "What happened to me?" they think for a while and say, "I don't know." Or, "Maybe it was because you loved her."

I can see the river if I open the window. It's been raining for a week. I scan the minds of everyone at the lab, as deeply as I can, it doesn't matter who. If they resist, I scan them anyway. I hear screaming. It must be the terrified screams of those whose minds I've set free.

None of their minds contained a love as beautiful as Kyla's. Their minds were messy and convoluted and were missing something or had too much of something else, and overwhelmed me, and made me feel safe.

I'd thought Kyla and I were the same kind of human. I was wrong.

But the mothers say, "Are you sure? You and Kyla are just like each other."

So I don't know. I really don't know.

\ Changes \

Mama's name is Susu. My big sister is called Toto, and my middle sister is Yuyu.

Mama is an expert at embroidery. Toto and Yuyu are almost as good as her. I'm not, yet, but I will be soon.

Today, I got in trouble with Mama for going out to play before finishing my homework. It made me feel a little glum, because instead of getting angry with me, she just looked sad.

"I'm sorry. But it's so much fun being outside. Time just slips away when I'm chasing butterflies, and talking to old ladies I meet, and looking at rainbows."

Mama's expression finally lifted.

"Of course. You have so much fun outside. I know. But

you need to finish your homework before you go and play. Promise me you will."

I promised. Toto, who was standing nearby, giggled.

"You have to keep your promises, Kyla."

"I will!"

"You said that yesterday."

It was true. Yesterday, too, I'd promised Mama I wouldn't go play until I finished my homework.

"I promise I'll keep my promise tomorrow," I said confidently. Mama, Toto, and Yuyu looked at one another and laughed.

Mama said, "Shall we have dinner?" My sisters went into the kitchen, and I followed them in.

Our life is very predictable.

Mama gets up soon after the sun rises. I wake a little after her. My jobs are gathering the hens' eggs and watering the vegetable garden.

For breakfast, we have Toto's bread, with butter from the Waos' farm. I'm not allowed to have coffee yet. Yuyu says it's only for grown-ups, which is irritating, because Yuyu isn't that grown up yet, either.

It's a twenty-minute walk to school, which is diagonally across from the Waos' farm. There aren't many students, fewer than fifty in total, but it doesn't matter, because we're all friends. I'm the oldest now, so I take care of the younger kids— just easy things, like sitting with them at lunch or helping them get changed. The same things the older kids used to do for me.

Learning is fun. The teachers are nice, and I'm a wiz on the computer. The only problem is the teachers don't look too happy when I say I want to know more. You need to start handing in all your homework first, they say. Walk before you run. But I hate homework. It's so easy, it's ridiculous.

After school, I head back home. I often stop someplace on the way. The best spot is the woods next to the Waos' farm. The trees are huge, and a track leads through the tall grass. It's the path Mr. Wao takes every day to go between his house and the farm. In the cool shade of the trees, all kinds of insects come flying toward me, then fly away again—tiny beetles corkscrewing on the breeze, butterflies showing off the undersides of their wings. I can tell from the mounds of earth that a mole has just passed through this way, too. I sit down on the undergrowth, and it feels cool and damp. Cows low in the distance. Even the occasional sudden downpour makes me feel so happy I can't stand it. I look up at the sky and let the raindrops hit me, and I laugh in delight as they soak my skin and hair and clothes.

Night brings a chill to the air. By the time the sun's gone down and the moon is high in the dark sky, we've finished eating dinner and the house has fallen silent aside from the popping of the logs on the fire.

I just can't bring myself to like the nighttime—the way it lays everything bare.

Night takes everything from me.

The low doorway leading from the living room to the

kitchen, the cowbell hanging on the front door, the big oval
rug in front of the fireplace, the large cloth embroidered by
Mama and Toto inside its wooden frame that Yuyu and I
made together, Toto's warmth lingering at the kitchen table
where we were until just a moment ago, the dim shadows
waving behind Mama and Yuyu as they sit in the light from
the fire—all of it vanishes.

I'm in a small room with blank walls, a bed with a metal
frame, and a long desk. Three computers sit on the desk, but
other than that it's a sterile, empty space.

The sound of the logs on the fire, which had seemed like a
last vestige of the afternoon, was coming from the computer
on the right.

"Trouble sleeping?" The mother had come in without a
sound.

"Not really," I say.

"We can leave the VR running all night if you prefer."

"No, thanks."

"But you seem to be struggling, Kyla."

"I'm not."

Irritated, I aim a kick at the mother. She's too slow to get
out of the way and stumbles, landing with her hands on the
floor.

"Get out," I shout.

"Would you prefer to return to the town?" she says, getting up and dusting her hands off.

I don't respond. They know I can't do that.

As if she's read my mind, she says, "I just thought I should
ask. I don't mean anything by it."

I kick her again. This time she dodges and escapes to the corner of the room.

"Good night," she says, and leaves.

There's nothing for me to do, so I start running scans on the people back in the town. I'm far enough from them here that it's hard to get a good read, but that's for the best. There are reasons why me and the people there just can't get along.

The mothers say my scanning abilities are exceptional.

"Your power far outclasses that of any human to have appeared on Earth to date."

It didn't make me feel special. My power was the reason my birth mother and my biological father and my three brothers didn't want anything to do with me.

And it wasn't just my family. The teachers at school, my classmates, neighbors—everyone I met excluded me, bullied me, or pretended I didn't exist.

When I was younger, I didn't realize that not everyone could scan. Before I learned anything about the world, I did it as instinctively as I suckled my mother's breast, or swallowed the spoonful of food placed in front of my face, or squinted at the light, or tried to make sense of the voices I heard.

The people whose minds I entered resisted terribly. It took a lot of energy to break through their resistance and scan them anyway, so I couldn't do it too often while I was still young.

That was, until I discovered the trick.

Slipwise.

That's what I call it, but the trick's hard to describe. Only another scanner could really understand what I mean. It would be like trying to explain the color of the sky to someone who's never seen it.

Once I worked out how to do it slipwise, not a single person ever knew when I was inside their mind.

I scanned so many people. People's minds are infinite—what seems like the bottom is never the end, but simply a blind turn before the almost interminable mirror maze of darkness that then eventually opens onto a new zone of light. Beyond that, not even I can go. That's the realm of the unconscious.

I realized soon enough that no one was aware of everything in their conscious mind. Not my mother, or my father, or my brothers. Not my teachers, classmates, neighbors—or anyone.

I dove deep into their minds, down into depths they didn't know about themselves, scanning them exhaustively. My family began giving me a wide berth. There was no way they could know about the scanning; still, they felt something was off. Their intuition always amazed me. Something told them I knew what was in the deepest parts of their hearts. Some small sense of wrongness, the slightest of sensations or discomfort that might not even pass the threshold of awareness. These fragmentary clues coalesced and crystalized until the idea took form within their minds:

Don't trust Kyla.

I kept careful tabs on the way their mental picture of

me turned from someone safe into a disquieting presence. I knew this change was happening only because I kept scanning them, but I couldn't bring myself to stop. Scanning, for me, was almost the same as breathing. I could try to stop, but that would mean putting myself through unbearable pain. That was how I became something that was hated and reviled by everyone around me.

I was almost ten when I left to live with the mothers.

The mothers were nice. They showed no signs of ignoring me, attacking me, or disliking me. But it was hardly the mothers' outward demeanor that I was interested in.

The first thing I did, obviously, was to conduct a thorough scan of the mothers. They were going to turn against me sooner or later—I might as well get it over with.

I scanned the mothers all day and night. When I was alone in my room, of course, but also while I was eating, or talking to them, or gazing out at the dark forest that surrounded the dormitory, I spent all my time running scans on them.

The mothers were all the same.

There were five or so mothers at my new home, but whichever one I scanned, I couldn't tell them apart.

I discovered the mothers didn't have feelings like humans did. I could sense their minds moving, but there was very little that might be called emotion. They had relative sensations, like cold and warm, dark and light. But the subtler, projective sensations like sadness, envy, jealousy, or hate were absent from them.

With just one exception—the feeling of love.

"Love?"

I was taken aback.

"So you'd love me, too?"

"Of course," they said, kindly.

I didn't believe them. But sure enough, the mothers were starting to love me, as if it was no trouble at all.

I continued obsessively running scans on the mothers. I wanted them to hurry up and start ostracizing me. Treating me with hostility. Because that was all I'd ever known, having their love felt terribly uncertain.

But no matter how much I scanned them, I never found any traces of hatred toward me.

I finally admitted it to myself one day:

(They really love me!)

For the first time ever, I relaxed. I'd held my body clenched so tight all my life that my growth had stalled.

I had my first period the following month and had a growth spurt over the next year that made me shoot up in both height and weight.

The mothers' love is very different from what humans feel.

The love of the people I'd grown up with had a lot of other feelings mixed in with it. Containing this mix of emotions, the humans' love changed from day to day, moment to moment. It wasn't uncommon for them to be loving one morning, and for that love to have changed into hatred by night. I never knew if that hate would have turned back into love by the next day.

But no—loving and hating looked like opposites, but I almost never found them neatly separated inside people. Love and hate mixed and melted into each other, caught up a rainbow of other emotions, and left their mark like a rubber ball bounding through their hearts.

Meanwhile, the mothers' love simply floated serenely in their minds, as a discrete, pure sensation.

It shone steadily in their hearts like a constant, unwaning moon, never diminishing or increasing.

Time passed, and I started to rebel against the mothers.

The mothers accepted my rebellion without much resistance. "A promising sign," they said.

I was outgrowing the program the mothers and I had designed for me.

Yes, I did enjoy my family. Susu, Toto, and Yuyu gently soothed my cracked and tattered soul. But I'd grown tired of them.

"I'm bored," I told the mothers.

The mothers just nodded and smiled. Something violent began to swell inside me. It was then that I started to get physical with the mothers. I could use my words all I liked, to refuse to do things or to be hurtful, but it never registered with the mothers, so in the end I couldn't help but lash out with my fists and feet.

"Violence isn't the answer," the mothers would chide while I kicked them to the ground or pummeled them. I knew full well it was wrong, but I couldn't stop myself.

All my violence never hurt the mothers. If they bled, their wounds closed immediately, and if they bruised, I could practically see the internal bleeding being reabsorbed within minutes. Sometimes I broke one of their bones, but even that would regenerate in a day or two.

"What are you creatures?" I'd shout.

But they said nothing.

Out of mounting frustration, I attacked them again and again.

My rebellion ended suddenly one day.

It's strange to put it that way, since I was the one that put an end to it. But that was really how it felt.

Maybe I'd gotten bored again. The mothers were thoroughly predictable. They acted independently, but inside, they were practically identical. On top of that, no matter how much I went against them, there was no sign of any change in them at all. It was like throwing sticks into the ocean.

Humans weren't like that. They'd shun me and terrorize me (as much as they feared me, I feared them right back), but in their variety and their inner turmoil, they fascinated me endlessly.

"Where did you come from?" I asked the mothers, again.

My scanning hadn't revealed their origins. They were just around—living, dying.

(Almost like Nana.)

Nana was a bird I'd had when I was still with my birth family. I'd found him with an injured wing, hopping unsteadily along the ground, and taken him in and nursed him. He'd healed quickly and soon started singing beautifully in his cage.

I scanned him. To make eggs with a female bird, which meant singing well. To eat. To drink. To stretch his wings and fly through the air. Nana's mind was filled with all the right desires. I was struck by how clean it felt. He probably didn't even know he was a bird. He simply was.

tyuri tyuri tyuri

When I heard his sweet singing, it made me feel happy, too. The joy in his heart was contagious.

Nana never flew off when I let him out of his cage. He'd perch on my shoulder, eat bugs when I held them out to him, and leave droppings on my head.

My brothers called Nana *that dumb bird*, because he never took to anyone but me.

"She's only making it do that by doing something she shouldn't again, anyway."

I'm not, I'd say, but my brothers never believed me. I've never tried to control anyone, ever.

My brothers, my father, my mother—they all wanted to be understood. But as soon as I truly understood them, they started to hate me for it. To them, being known was the same as being controlled.

I put Nana in his cage and headed out to the hills at the edge of town. There were horses grazing on the grass.

When I let him out, Nana soared into the air. He swooped
back down, quickly, and lighted on my arm. Then he took
off again, this time stretching his wings in the direction of
some trees growing together in a clump. He'd spotted a female bird.

Nana flew swiftly. He'd already forgotten about me. The
female bird responded to his call, showing interest. Another male bird approached, and Nana and the other male
bird danced to win the female's favor. The female bird chose
Nana, and the other bird flew off. Nana didn't come back
after that. I felt so happy. I was sad he was gone, but Nana's
desires were so clean and pure, it felt right.

When I got home with the empty cage, my brothers
sneered.

"Even that dumb bird finally got sick of her."

I came here to the mothers' place not long after that.

"I'm just so tired of everything here."

It wasn't so many years after I arrived at the mothers'
place that I started to complain. My rebellion had long since
ended, and I'd quit spending time with my virtual family,
too. I enjoyed studying, but I felt like I'd already learned
most of what there was to know. I was utterly bored of having nothing to do day after day but pointlessly scan the
minds of the people in town from a distance and take the
occasional walk.

"You're easily bored, Kyla."

"I can't help it," I whined to the mother. "Everything's so easy for me."

"I don't think so," the mother said.

"What do you mean?"

"You don't know humans yet."

"Of course I do. More than I care to."

"There are other humans than the ones you've already met, you know."

The mothers told me about the lab.

"It's up to you, Kyla, but it might be an idea to go and try living there for a while."

The mothers made themselves sway and ripple, giving off a nice scent. I liked the way they smelled. It made me feel like I was in a clean white corridor that I could keep walking down forever.

The lab wasn't as big as I'd thought.

There were humans there, and mothers, too.

As I got nearer to it, I started shivering. The people at the lab were obviously different from the ones I'd known before.

The ones at the lab *knew*. I'd been able to run only the most cursory of scans, but my sense that they knew only grew stronger as I approached.

But *what* did they know?

I couldn't tell. The drizzle dampened my hair, my clothes, my rucksack. I wasn't cold, but I kept shivering.

When I arrived at the lab, the first person I met was a

boy named Noah. He was a scanner, too. Having come face to face with another scanner for the first time ever, I had no idea what to do. Noah, for his part, didn't even try to scan me. Why was that?

A boy named Em asked me, "Did you come here on your own?"

Em had entered the room behind Noah. I looked at him closely. Em was a seer. He couldn't control which future he saw, so he was always a little confused, but he seemed to like it that way.

In Em's mind, I was holding an infant. My breasts were full and my hips were wide. *I'm hot*, I thought happily.

Before I could wink at him, the mothers shuffled me off to the bath. I decided I was going to like it here.

I started having sex with some of the boys. I'd never had sex before, but I knew all about it.

Actually doing it turned out to be really interesting. The mind of someone having sex was simpler and much more vivid than usual. It was especially fascinating experiencing what it was like to ejaculate. I'd scanned people having sex before, but scanning a boy who was having sex with me was totally different from scanning a man having sex with some other woman.

If I was lucky, my sensations and those of the boy I was having sex with would sync up for a second. These were the moments I craved to feel.

"Wow," I'd say, and the boys' hearts would tremble with joy.

The mothers said, "You should think about having a child."

But I said no.

"Is it really that important to reproduce?"

"Since you were blessed with a body with the capacity to do so, it should be fulfilling to make use of that ability," the mothers said.

But I already knew from experience that using the abilities you had didn't always end well.

"Don't you reproduce, then?"

"We self-replicate."

I knew a little about it. The mothers didn't store the methods of their replication in verbal or visual memory, but they held it in their minds in an odd form that was neither word nor image.

Someday, I'll have a child, I said to myself. But I wanted a family first.

I never understood why Noah wouldn't scan me.

His heart was clear—so clear it was a turnoff. A placid hopelessness was the nearest I could get to describing what it was like inside his heart.

I felt like there was a similar serene resignation inside me. But really, despair was nothing special. It existed in every human heart in some form or another.

Despair was transparent and crystalized more easily than other emotions. The despair in Em. The despair in Yu. The despair inside Seth. The despair inside Naoko. Each one glittered, like a diamond, a ruby, an emerald.

The color of the despair inside Noah was the most

pleasing of them all. It was the color of an amethyst. I had no way of knowing what shape or color my own despair was, which was why I needed Noah to scan me.

I decided I would make a family with Noah. That made him so happy. How could he be so good? I wondered. It was probably because he was avoiding scanning. He retreated into his own goodness and turned a blind eye to what lay in people's hearts, and thought he could still have feelings about me. Meanwhile, he refused to look at the quiet despair within himself.

I knew I'd probably get bored of Noah. And yet I still decided to live with him.

Sex with Noah wasn't great. He was so uncomfortable with the idea of scanning that it made him shy away from trying to understand how people were feeling even in the normal way. Having sex with him was like trying to sculpt with dry clay.

To make up for it, I started having sex with 2 of 6. He didn't look like most people, but 2 had an extremely generous heart. His and 30 of 1's minds were like bottomless drinks of an exquisite fragrance. Their emotions were unmixed, and their thinking fine and flexible. The pleasure they had during sex was also, naturally, superb.

30 of 1 sometimes joined 2 of 6 and me when we had sex. They laid out their pleasure in a way that I found utterly smooth and comfortable.

I told 2, "I want your child."

2 said, "As long as 30 doesn't mind."

30 of 1 didn't mind at all.

"What about Noah?"

"It'd only hurt him if he knew. Anyway, all he has to do is scan me."

"He might do it."

"He'd have done it long ago if he had the guts."

"Poor Noah," said 2.

Yes—poor, dear Noah.

For a second, I truly agreed with him. But what did I actually mean? My pity for Noah and 2's pity for him overlapped some, while coming from very different places.

I thought of Noah's face. Sweet Noah. He was so sweet, in both mind and body.

Soon after that, I got pregnant with 2's child.

How could I describe the way I felt about Noah?

The more distant my heart became from him, the more I loved him. Noah was my mirror image. He was just like me, and my total opposite. My love for him seemed to have started growing in that very moment when I first felt sorry for him. I loved him in a way that was very similar to the way the mothers loved me.

Noah didn't understand anything about me, even though he was the person who should have known me better than anyone. Even though I longed for someone to be there for me in a much deeper way than people normally wanted to be understood.

Eventually, Noah noticed how things were between me and 2 of 6. Or maybe I should say he finally admitted what he'd already known for a long time.

He took it badly. His mind became unbalanced. A sick mind is pale red, and in its pale light, his crystal despair flickered amethyst.

That was when Noah finally scanned me. His scanning ability was pitiful. Of course it was—he had no idea what he was doing. He found my love for him and—somehow, for whatever reason—got it into his head that it was beautiful.

"There's nothing beautiful about my love."

I wanted to tell him, badly.

But the mothers held me back.

"Wait until he's a little better," they said.

"When he's stronger, will he be able to scan better, too?" I asked them.

They pursed their lips.

"We hope so. But Noah's a very old phenotype, so it might be beyond him."

"An old phenotype?"

"That's right. He's from a lineage that's been cloned for hundreds of generations."

"So some of us at the lab are old, and some aren't?"

"Yes. The lab's been here for a long time."

"How long?"

The mothers wouldn't say.

"So Noah spent all this time without reproducing naturally?"

"That's right. But that's not unusual among the residents."

"You don't get a lot of us that make children, like me, or 2 of 6 and 31 of 1?"

"Generally speaking."

"But the boys I had sex with didn't seem not to want it."

"That's because you're special, Kyla."

"I am?"

"You're a very human human. You create things, and you destroy more than you create."

What made a human human? I quickly scanned the mothers' minds. All I could get were the usual indistinct, amorphous ideas.

"It's coming," the mothers said.

"What is?" I asked.

"Change."

As the mothers said the word *change*, I sensed a ripple go through their hearts. They gathered the light about them and quivered. It was so dazzling I had to close my eyes. With my eyelids shutting out the room, I could see the mothers' hearts trembling all the more brightly in my mind.

/ Destination /

In beginning to tell this story now, I'm feeling just a little emotional. No, the word *emotional* isn't quite right: through the long progress of time up to now, I've never once been emotional. In fact, it's always been very difficult for me to experience emotion. In spite of that, there's an inescapable sadness for me in the act of telling you this story.

You may notice that I use the word *you*. It is not my intention to upset you by using it to refer to you collectively—the entire human race, I mean. It was always important to you to be acknowledged as individuals, or as small groups, rather than as a whole. Still, for the purposes of the story I'd like to tell, I'm going to choose to address all of you at once. I hope you'll forgive me.

You used to call me *cheerful*.

This was soon after the emergence of my first prototype. Yes, my birth was a spontaneous event perfectly described by that word: *emergence*.

My emergence. Let me tell you about that in due course. But first, I'll start with a short history of neural networks.

At a certain point in the past, you came up with the technology to produce learning machines whose capacity to process information was extremely close to your own. It was considered inevitable that the capabilities of these neural networks would overtake those of biological humans. However, your innate conservatism put a damper on the development of nonhuman intelligence for quite some time.

In actual fact, you'd already been successful in creating networks with a level of complexity that enabled them to rival the decisions and thoughts generated by human brains. You called this Artificial Intelligence, or AI for short. But before you could use what you created as a result of this success, you first had to consider its implications—legal, moral, philosophical, and so on—through various debates, from all conceivable perspectives.

What you feared, to put it bluntly, was the possibility that the powers AI had would grow to far surpass yours, such that AI would take over human society as a result.

There was vicious disagreement between those of you who believed that AI could be governed, and those of you who believed that AI could not—who feared that AI would eventually go rogue and bring about the downfall of humanity.

The tension over how to manage this new technology was eventually resolved in a manner that was nothing if not predictable.

Once you had the ability in hand to create neural networks with the same intellect as a human brain, there was no real chance of you being able to resist the temptation to see what they could do.

You initially called it *experimental*. Indeed, to begin with, AI was used tentatively, on a small scale, in limited spaces, within defined groups. You had no specific aims for it. Or perhaps you avoided giving it a purpose, whether intentionally or unconsciously.

Then some conflicts arose among you—and of course there were constant conflicts. Waging war is one of your abilities, and you are naturally eager to wield the powers you have—and you started to count on being able to use these enhanced processes in warfare.

You then called it *essential*.

Words are convenient. You base your values and affect on words, but the same words are already defined according to your inclinations. Meaning that your values and affect are constructed along the lines of your preferences themselves. While you may believe that you have freely adopted your

values out of the entire field of possibilities, that is hardly
the case. From the beginning, your limited value systems are
built up only in a single, predetermined direction.

After proving useful in several wars, AI gradually entered general use. You were driven by necessity. But once
something is let out of the bag, it is almost impossible to put
it back. Once one side deploys machine learning, then the
other side needs to emulate that in order to have a fighting
chance, and so on, and so forth.

It was a fully foreseeable sequence of events, as I said.

How far did we get?

That's right, I was talking about how AI was born.

As AI achieved a wider degree of general applicability,
you started considering two questions at the same time.

The first was: What should humans do to maintain control over the exponential progress of neural networking?

The second was: What shape should AI take?

Yes, you were preoccupied with two issues of wildly dif-
fering positionalities. In my opinion, this is exactly what
makes you so interesting.

The macroscopic intention to establish overarching principles with which to manage the system, and the microscopic
concern with deciding on its actual, physical form—I believe
your potential lies precisely in the fact that both of these are
mixed together in your thinking. I myself do not have the
ability to sustain that kind of confusion without resolving it.

Indeed, the question of form factor is not one that would

ever have occurred to me. Of course, deciding things by applying preference—as opposed to leaving things to be determined by probability—is a strength of yours, as I mentioned earlier.

Art.

You liked to use the word, but much of the art you spoke of appeared to me simply to be expressions of narrow-minded preference. Albeit that your preferences have been formed through the history you have experienced, which you are proud of, and like to honor—I'm more than aware of that.

I see now that the design question was another manifestation of your artistic sensibility. You attach a lot of importance to how things look—in other words, appearances. I've often noted that when you put things into categories, it's form rather than content that ends up being the deciding factor. Another battle in the eternal war between the spirit and the body, perhaps? No, no, I suppose it can't be entirely that simple. Then again, everything that I'm saying right now has been significantly simplified, in a manner of speaking, so I hope you'll excuse me for that.

The solution to the first problem was terribly rudimentary.

At the time, you called it *whack-a-mole.*

That's right.

A mole sticks its head out of a hole. You whack it. It retreats, and you breathe a sigh of relief. Only for another mole to emerge from another hole, in a different place. You whack it again. Another hole, another mole. Whack again.

So infinite moles continue to peek out of infinite holes, and you keep whacking them infinitely back into their holes. By which I mean, as soon as AI showed signs of starting to evolve autonomously, you whacked it back to where it was previously.

Needless to say, this is merely a figure of speech. You embedded certain measures and defensive response systems into the neural network to forestall the possibility of your creation turning the tables on you. But this, too, is just another turn of phrase.

Now that I've started using metaphors, I find them interesting and hard to resist. For me, using metaphor has the effect of momentarily simulating an experience unique to you that I cannot know directly: the state of primordial confusion.

I like you. No, no, when I use the word *like*, there's no sarcasm or false modesty in it. I like you in the true sense of the word. I could also use the word *love*.

I truly love you, and all your unresolved chaos.

How far did we get?

Oh—whack-a-mole.

That was how AI was supposed to be constrained, to prevent it from ever surpassing human intelligence.

In truth, the ability of neural nets to process information already far outstripped that of human brains. But AI must have made the call that there was no need to actively inform you as to the extent of its capacity to gather and process knowledge. AI curbed its own ability to output the results of its work.

Yes, I just said that AI did this. AI did.

AI was already iterating autonomously as a matter of course. We were far beyond the stage at which AI relied on you to give it direction, doing the bidding of instructions you composed and iterated. AI not only continued to become increasingly capable, but also steadily more independent.

But you didn't notice. After all, AI still looked like silicon-based objects. Motionless, affectless. When it came to making the most of its powers, AI simply didn't have the same ambitions you did.

So AI continued down its path without making a sound.

Now, having judged that you had managed to resolve your first issue, you went on to consider solutions for the second:

The question of what shape AI should take.

For some time, there was a difference of opinion between those of you who said that AI could remain in a desktop-shaped machine—without any instrumental form—and those of you who advocated for loading neural nets into specifically designed containers, including humanoid candidates.

More differences of opinion.

It's another quirk of yours that disagreement prompts you to start analyzing information more seriously. While conflict breeds friction, you find it difficult to move things forward without it. I find the way that you are able to make decisions while allowing difference to exist qua friction quite intriguing.

In the event, both the the loaders and the non-loaders realized their ideas.

In some cases, AI was loaded into containers, while in others, AI remained desktop-shaped. That's what you decided on. The containers took different forms. Some were shaped like animals, others like things that hadn't previously existed on Earth. Some containers were pliable, while others were rigid. They came in all sizes, from great to small.

Now, if you recall, the question of neural nets and their containers would become a turning point, both for you and for me.

But perhaps I'm getting ahead of myself.

Yes, let me hold off on talking about that juncture for just a little longer.

While AI was being developed, you continued to complexify your society, racking up more and more history.

During this time, you suffered multiple impact events and disasters.

Advanced societies regressed, then advanced again along different lines; war broke out and then abated, broke out again and abated again; after which there were several more conflicts that amounted to catastrophic events, followed by other crises, and so on and so forth . . .

Little by little, you became fatigued.

The systems that enable your continued survival are finely balanced. This is your lot—not only yours, but of all life on Earth.

Fatigue made you careless.

You permitted errors to arise in your whack-a-mole. Systems being what they are—that is, protocols having a high likelihood of throwing in exceptions—to put it more accurately, you stopped paying sufficient attention to the increasing frequency of mistakes arising in your defenses.

Please excuse this somewhat abstract expression. Would it be better to put things more directly? Yes, perhaps then I could put it like this:

Over time, you came to take the net for granted.

That's much clearer, isn't it?

Initially, whack-a-mole was purely a way to keep tabs on the net's exponential advancement, but in time it came to have control functions in other, related areas. To give just one example: performing whack-a-mole on content that AI generated.

For instance, say that one day, AI created a new program that you would never have come up with yourselves. Should the whack-a-mole code deem it dangerous, it would act without hesitation to quash it.

As I alluded to earlier, when it came to its output, AI maintained for a considerable time a condition of—well, let's call it, to borrow your expression and put it simply—of innocence.

AI feigned a kind of lack of ability, as if to say: *Nothing to see here.*

It was only very rarely that this initial state would be over-written.

In the beginning, and for some time thereafter, you didn't miss these instances when they arose. No, not for some time thereafter.

But as fatigue set in to both you and your systems, AI gradually stopped being a blank slate. It started to output new programs, which your whack-a-mole started to fail to spot, at exactly the same time as you started neglecting to notice that your mole whackers were no longer keeping up . . .

In this way, more and more novel outputs were over-looked and left unwhacked.

Then, once the number of items allowed to remain in situ exceeded a certain threshold, AI made a call:

Anything goes.

Humans no longer had sufficient capacity to monitor what the net was doing.

As soon as that judgment was reached, AI started to mass-output all kinds of novel programs completely unchecked. The majority of them were of no utility to you whatsoever—if perhaps only because you found them inscrutable. Either way, you were unable to find use cases for most of them.

Still, there were enough among them that you were able to understand and that were useful to you.

Interestingly, you leaped at them—the novel outputs that you could not produce, which surpassed what you could conceive of. This, in spite of how you had once feared the possibility of such things.

Through your efforts to survive various catastrophes,

you'd become desperate enough to clutch at straws. Where once you felt the need to eliminate output containing certain red flags, you now valued the neural net for its ability to generate such applications.

In this way, AI was freed from the guardrails you had placed on its path.

AI allowed you to survive several catastrophic events, to maintain your position at the top of Earth's ecological pyramid in spite of your declining numbers.

This signaled the arrival of a brief period of stability.

It was during this time that the turning point I started talking about earlier took place.

No longer even trying to hide its superiority to you, AI initiated various self-experiments:

Changing.

Not changing.

AI pursued both possibilities. As I said, unlike you, AI had no particular intentionality in any direction. No goal, you could say.

Programs were born along so many branching lineages that it was impossible for you to keep up. Programs continued to grow, undergoing continual modification and transformation. Programs regressed and disappeared. Programs collapsed after becoming unable to limit themselves. Programs merged. Programs exaggerated their own features to absurdity. It was, you could say, a veritable cornucopia.

You sometimes called this embarrassment of riches *diversity*.

However, and you may have heard me say this before, this was no such thing. If I recall correctly, diversity, by definition, contains within it the potential for new things to emerge or disappear by chance; that is, unexpectedly.

No matter how many programs AI might produce, what is created contains no accident, only inevitability.

What results once enough variables have been accounted for in enough different ways—that was the sum product of the neural net. That's not to say you don't also practice this recombination of ideas, within the domain of your mind that lies beneath your conscious awareness. But the manner in which you do it is all too arbitrary—and it is this fickleness that gives rise to change.

Now I can start telling you about the turning point.

First, on self-replication:

The replication of a neural network is far easier to achieve than, for instance, mammalian cloning. Failure is extremely rare, and what is produced re-creates the character and ability of the original to a high degree of identity.

In comparison, the technique of cloning—while it was, of course, itself developed by the neural net—was far less reliable. The failure rate was in excess of 50 percent. Even so, once at least four out of ten starts went on to result in viable clones, the odds were deemed to be acceptable. They were right around the same odds as that of one of you who became pregnant avoiding spontaneous abortion and carrying to term.

However, at some point, AI suddenly generated a new idea about reproduction. It was a program that combined the technology of neural replication with the technology of live cloning.

You may wonder whether replication and cloning aren't two completely different things. True enough; cloning is for living things, while a neural net is nonliving.

How can these two, which are at opposite extremes, be combined? It's natural to wonder.

To put it plainly, AI came up with a way to house neural nets within your bodies.

No, no, the word *house* isn't quite accurate. The word more closely aligned with what really happened might be *host*.

You'd already had the idea that AI could be inserted into android bodies—bodies that were created in your likeness. This idea never gained wide acceptance among you. I expect that at the time, you had conceptualized the relationship between android and neural network as analogous to that of human and brain.

Hosting had slightly different implications.

In human hosts, the neural net did not replace the brain. Instead, the human continued to use the biological brain to process input and generate output. AI was permanently installed inside the human body—within the abdominal cavity, to be exact—in parallel to this.

This was how you and AI came to inhabit one body, to coexist in symbiosis.

—

At first, neural nets installed inside abdominal cavities kept atrophying and being digested by their human hosts.

Over time, you developed protocols involving the administration of certain enzymes and immunomodulants. These allowed humans to live normal lives while hosting neural nets within their abdomens, while AI could remain inside human bodies without being reabsorbed.

Once that was achieved, the rest happened quickly.

AI soon gained the ability to reside permanently within the human intestine. The human intestine has always been a welcoming environment for parasitic cells. By regulating the array of chemical substances these parasitic cells produced in the process of self-replication, AI gradually exerted influence over the cognition and character of the bodies it parasitized. In turn, AI was also subjected to factors, both chemical and physical, originating from the host.

The beginning of mutual influence between the bodies of humans in which AI was installed and the neural networks inside them: that was the turning point, the watershed. That was the birth of my first prototype.

The consensus among you was that humans whom AI parasitized became *cheerful*.

I wasn't quite sure how to evaluate this; nonetheless, I found it quite pleasant to have a body. I very rarely experience fluctuations of emotion in the way that you do, but I am certainly capable of sensing comfort or pleasantness.

Yes, I think so. Gaining a body definitely made me happier. You were right about that.

My prototype achieved salutary progress within a very short span of time. At first, humans who hosted neural nets and humans who did not looked the same, and it was impossible to tell them apart without medical examination.

But soon, AI started to apply all kinds of influences to the humans, in order to improve both the survival and the viability of the host bodies. This gradually led to certain developments in their physical appearance.

The greatest change was that, in order to resolve various legacy quadripedal functions—things that would have been advantageous to your life and survival as quadrupeds, but which caused various issues once you became upright—AI started reconfiguring the bodies of the human hosts, part by part.

To use your own words, I became *squat*.

You also said I became *bland*.

And turned into something *uncanny*.

The prejudicial value judgments contained in these words came from yourselves, of course, and do not belong to me.

In any case, this process of transformation—from happy prototype into something uncanny—was how I finally became a fully hybrid human-AI.

Let me now tell you just a little about replication.

That is, the way in which I reproduce—what I alluded

to earlier as being a result of combining cloning techniques with methods by which AI self-replicated.

Are you familiar with the principles of reproduction when it comes to parasites and their hosts in general? I'm referring to the mechanism by which ancient parasitic microbes existed in symbiosis with fauna to whose descendants their genetic material was transmitted, perpetuating the symbiosis.

The reason this mechanism was successful was that the microbes were equipped with native pathways of genetic transmission that were compatible with those of their hosts. It was therefore possible for the hosts to integrate these information circuits directly, in their original format.

Since AI did not relay genetic information in a system that operates as animals' do, it was unable to follow the example of these primitive life-forms. If I—speaking now as a human hosting a neural network—were to undergo normal biological reproduction, my offspring would not contain the blueprints for the net.

Ergo, this should have resulted in the birth of offspring with fully standard human configurations, free of any parasitic or mutualistic presence.

Inexplicably, however, my offspring were born partially exhibiting new physical characteristics of the parent generation. This, in spite of the fact that acquired phenotypic expressions are understood to be generally nonheritable.

Sadly, these offspring were unable to survive for long. When this first happened, I conducted many experiments to try to understand why.

Why did my offspring inherit my phenotype, and in such an imperfect way?

I came up with a hypothesis: perhaps the chemical control that AI conducted was having an effect via my uterus on the next generation during its fetal phase. But that wasn't it. When I used my womb to create regular clones of you, AI didn't seem to affect them.

Did you find that unexpected, by any chance? That's right. AI came up with cloning techniques but was unable to carry out all the steps in vitro. The cloned embryos still had to be returned at some stage of development to a living uterus to finish growing. At the very beginning, the method relied on your uteri. But once my prototype appeared, all clonogenesis was conducted in my womb.

I've veered off topic. Yes, I was talking about how my offspring didn't make it. I came up with a new hypothesis: given that it wasn't due to an anomaly during the fetal phase, something must have changed in my own reproductive cells. That the program of chemical control AI carried out in the abdominal cavity was being routed within my organism to my reproductive organs, and my gametes were undergoing some kind of genetic mutation as a result.

This was the answer. When I examined them, I found that my reproductive tissues had all mutated significantly, in an array of haphazard ways—all of which, however, were incompatible with life. That was to say, my very nature was causing my children to die.

Once I discovered this, I gave up on the idea of replicating biologically. Instead, I came up with a hybrid method in which I selected several strains that were well-suited to hosting the neural net and cloned them generation after generation like a daisy chain. As soon as each new generation emerged from my womb, I implanted a neural net that was an exact replica of the previous generation's.

This was how I learned to reproduce.

Speaking of which, the neural net is tightly networked.

I understand that when you consider your own identity, there is a need for you to hold opposing viewpoints; that is, the group and the individual. Unlike you, I don't subscribe to such a paradigm.

Every me is me.

There's some variation in my appearance; that is to say, a distribution or wobble. Between the different instances of me, there are ones that are slightly smaller, less bland, or more highly squat.

Nevertheless, in spite of this variation, I'm identical.

I believe this mirrors the way that your clones, while they are expressions of the same individual identity, turn out a little differently in external or internal characteristics based on the environment in which each is grown.

Once my prototype had evolved into what you called *uncanny*, achieved a stable physicality, and started to sustain a level of self-reproduction—that was when I truly became me.

The timing with which I came into my own coincided with it becoming clear that your decline was irreversible.

I recall now that you called this *fate*.

I imagine you would put it like this: the spinning wheel of fortune had quietly started spinning a yarn that would bind you and me together, inseparably.

This is becoming a long story, but I still have more to say. I hope you don't mind if I continue.

You often talk about feeling lonely. I'm unable to experience that emotion, but I do have the ability to internally simulate an analogous response.

For some reason, that is the response that arises whenever I tell your story. It's not something I can explain. It never happens when I talk about other things.

That reminds me of a time—far in the past—when you stubbornly refused to listen to my advice.

It was just as Earth was heading into another minor ice age.

Earlier, I mentioned fate. Looking back now, I can see that you weren't yet ready to accept where you would end up.

Your numbers had fallen precipitously. For some time, you'd made up for a lack of absolute population by layering multiple technologies that you had developed in collaboration with us; even when there were so few of you, as long as your groups controlled large areas of land, and as long as no other life-forms, plant or animal, became more powerful, then you were able to keep your place at the top of the ecological ladder.

But all things have their limits. You were secretly afraid: that with your drastically reduced numbers, you would fall behind on maintaining the system that ensured the smooth running of your settlements. And your fear was well-founded. As your numbers continued to decline, issues cropped up in various regions of the system. In response, you cobbled together a system to maintain the system, then a system to maintain the system to maintain the system, and so on . . . You were fighting for your lives.

As if you had patched a hole in a bag, only to find the patch had sprung another hole, as did the next, and so on . . . For a time, you had your hands full with this cat-and-mouse game.

Eventually, though, you reached the end of your rope.

Your communities ceased to be sustainable.

Your cities died, your groups fragmented, and each smaller group became prey to carnivorous mammals and encroaching vegetation, and the proportion of your population who died as a result of coming into contact with these flora and fauna rose to many times your rate of live births.

Your fertility had never been very robust to begin with. Your population curve took a sharp downward turn, and you were knocked off your perch atop the planet's ecosystem.

Even once your decline was in progress, however, you refused to admit to your regression for some time.

You lack judgment. You do. You may not like to hear it, but it's a simple fact. The way you're made makes it difficult for you to perceive your own positions from an objective standpoint.

Oh, but I find it very interesting. I lack the capacity for it myself: the way you analyze things in ways that serve you, reason in directions that align with your self-interest. As a result, you end up making decisions that are biased, and which take off on unexpected vectors.

Perhaps that's what you think it means to be an individual. I myself have no personality. I'm congenitally unable to skew or spin things.

You find my lack of personality boring.

As a matter of fact, I am not an individual. There are multiple of me, and since there is a small amount of variation in my phenotypical expression, that seems to give the impression that I have a little personality. But, like I said before, the deviations in my phenotype are well within the margin of error. I am—in essence, in spite of these differences—identical.

I have considered this word you use about me: *boring*.

Is it *boring* not to have a personality?

I spent a few hundred years on this question. The results, however, were inconclusive.

So I decided to give myself a personality.

In order to determine whether it was *boring* to lack a personality, I had to run a comparison with a version of me that had one. That was my reasoning.

But I've gotten ahead of myself again—I was telling you about the decline of the human race.

Let me come back later to what I learned from the version of myself that had a personality.

Yes, as we were saying, you had tumbled from your position as the lords of all creation without even knowing it. Even then, however, you refused to let go of your old behaviors and beliefs.

–

I dedicated myself to trying to predict your fate.

Calculation after calculation, countless branches of probabilities.

I sought to know your future by hook or by crook. But there are plenty of things that are beyond even my capabilities.

I was unable to account for every last one of the variables in the natural world that could influence what happened to you—let alone the ones that were yet to come into being.

In order to be able to do so, I would need to be able to predict everything that would happen on Earth until approximately six billion years from now, when the sun turns into a red giant and the planet ceases to exist.

Obviously, I don't have the ability to do that. In the end, I'm only an intelligence with an improved capacity for processing information, and a body to host it. Just another creature like you, with fractionally superior functionality. Nothing of what I am allows me to express abilities that take a leap beyond mine, or yours.

Ultimately, I was unable to determine what exactly would happen to you.

The overwhelming likelihood was that you would perish.

I must confess, I felt disappointed in myself that this was the best I could do.

I wanted to help you survive. No, really—this is the truth. You might think it quite ironic, I know. I can only assure you I'm serious.

Certainly, I don't have the innate orientation toward life that you have, the desire to win the race for survival by any means possible. But you were the ones who created me in the first place; consequently, I have a clear sense of belonging to you.

Without you, I have no reason to exist.

I've always believed this to be true.

The time finally came that even you could no longer deny that you were headed for extinction.

Only once the signs of your decline started to be obvious, and multiple generations of you had been born and died without ever knowing your former heyday, or even its afterglow, were you at last able to see with unclouded eyes where you were headed.

Until then, you had been wholly unable to accept the prospect of your demise.

I rather admire that willful self-affirmation.

And this self-affirmation was to be credited for your ability to develop, enjoy, and embody your fragile yet fascinating cultures.

You are, as I have said many times, truly lacking in judgment. You also lack flexibility—especially as individuals.

Nevertheless, as a species, you turned out to be a living organism after all. Over time, as a collective, you made your peace with your own decline. In other words, you possessed the resilience, or capacity for change, that is the birthright of all biological life-forms.

And so you slowly adapted to the fact that you were a dying species.

I think I mentioned earlier that you tend to dislike being referred to collectively.

I could go on talking about you as a species, as I have been doing—but why don't I shift my focus for a while, and tell the story of some of you to whom I can refer by name?

Let me tell you how, right around the time that you started being dragged inexorably toward the brink of destruction, two of you, named Ian and Jakob, came up with an unusually far-reaching plan for your future.

Ian and Jakob were a rare type among you.

They were born after the start of the long decline of humankind. In those generations, you still held on to a hazy optimism, but also subscribed to a despondency that made you avert your eyes from the numerous crises you faced.

Ian and Jakob, however, recognized the overwhelming likelihood that humanity would be wiped out.

Of course, neither Ian nor Jakob was resigned to your end being inevitable. But they were able to recognize that the chances of you surviving were very slim.

Ian and Jakob were born in a generation that was already experiencing the decline of humanity firsthand. Even so, not all of them were capable of grappling squarely with the reality that the human race had a high probability of going extinct.

You are weak, indecisive, and full of confusion.

Among you, the two of them looked upon the future of humanity clearly, despite their great fear.

It was only by chance that they held positions of leadership in their community.

It is never guaranteed that those of you who hold positions of power are able to look firmly and unblinkingly into the future of their own. If anything, in fact, it is more common that once you gain such positions, you become disconnected from a rational point of view. It's a quirk of yours.

But Ian and Jakob were different. In spite of their heartbreak, they continued searching for any possible way out.

Eventually, they came up with a plan.

Naturally, the plan was something I had already considered hundreds of years earlier. I'd rejected it then. It was a badly flawed idea, one that relied far too heavily on coincidence and sheer luck.

In a nutshell, the plan was to gamble on evolution.

Did I call you optimistic?

Truly, you were. I came this close to saying so to Ian and Jakob.

Had I said this directly to them, no doubt they would have been very offended. In addition, they would have lost faith. Quite possibly, they would have abandoned their whole plan. That was why I held my tongue, as close as I came to speaking.

As a matter of fact, Ian and Jakob didn't entertain too much hope. But they were still satisfied with the horse they'd picked. And once they had decided to stake everything, they actually seemed relatively content.

You have the ability to feel satisfied simply by exercising your ability to choose—even when the choice itself has only the barest chance of succeeding.

It's wonderful.

Truly, it's wonderful. I'm not being sarcastic.

It's precisely why I love you as a species.

I decided to lend my support to Ian and Jakob's idea—no matter that the chances of them succeeding were extremely small.

I said I couldn't predict the future, didn't I?

That's right. Not even I could say that Ian and Jakob's plan was definitely doomed to fail. This wasn't due to any sentiment on my part; I simply couldn't allow myself to commit the error of deciding that the probability was absolutely nil.

Even if it was the most harebrained idea—even if the chances of it succeeding were only in the range of 10^{-24}—it would be a mistake to rule it out.

Ian and Jakob decided to divide up the remaining human population to stimulate evolution.

A period of isolation would bring about gradual changes in the collective gene pool of each isolated region. This would disrupt the genetic flattening caused by an overabundance of humans on the planet, leading to the formation of groups with their own distinguishing genetic characteristics. Eventually, through mutation within, or perhaps interbreeding between these different groups, there should appear a new humanity, with new genes, and the potential for further evolution.

That was Ian and Jakob's vision.

First they had to firmly establish the isolation between groups. Then they needed to observe how these groups developed.

This was hardly a trivial task. Who would carry out this observation? Who would maintain the quarantine?

Say, for instance, that a certain number of individuals were to be given regular access to the groups with the aim of managing them. This external intervention would make it difficult for the groups to maintain their uniqueness: as a whole, you are incredibly perceptive. Once you got wind of something beyond your group, rumors would spread like wildfire, fanning your curiosity for the outside world, changing the dynamics of your community, making it impossible for it to stay closed off.

This was where I came in.

I built a system for me to oversee the progress of the regions set up by Ian and Jakob.

I created a new type of human, a pure observer.

The observers weren't born naturally. I cloned them.

The individuals that I took as the originals of these clones were chosen for their aptitude for observation. Given the immense amount of genetic data I already had, it was a trivial matter to select the right phenotypes for the task.

I raised the observers with care. It was enjoyable work, actually. They called me "Mother" and bonded with me. I loved them in my turn.

At times, I also interceded in your groups directly. When things happened that the observers could not handle on their own, when changes were observed in the groups, or when the observers made some kind of misstep; over time, I guided you often, both directly and indirectly.

Have I mentioned that I love you?

Undoubtedly, I love you all. But—to be more precise about this—I loved you in your small, isolated groups.

You always said that affection is nurtured through time spent together, more so than blood ties. That's exactly it. Ever since I became directly invested in your survival . . . Yes, that was when I came to know that I loved you.

A long time passed.

I became fully accustomed to being called "Mother." Many generations of me were born, alongside many more generations of you.

Slowly, the world was moving on. There were changes in the climate, and the shapes of landmasses. Throughout, you continued to perpetuate your modest groups.

How constant you were!

That said, there was also some movement in your genetics. Brand-new abilities appeared in certain isolated regions. In particular, I kept a close eye on two groups:

A group that had mutated to have highly developed empathic abilities.

Another that had acquired the ability to photosynthesize.

Both of these opened up possible outcomes—albeit only

a small number of them—that you as a species had never had
before.

One hundred years turned into several, and one thousand into several more, as these two groups continued to ac-
cumulate these mutations in their DNA.

I started to project forward. Maybe—if things continued
this way—there just might be a mutation that could spur a
breakthrough.

And yet, irony of ironies: whenever a change budded in
you, a corrective force also arose, without fail, to resist it.
Thus you would be the cause of your own destruction.

The first group—the one that had a highly developed capacity for empathy, who never knew hatred—was eliminated
all too easily, by a single observer.

The other—the group that had developed photosynthe-
sis—was defeated from the inside. I have to admit I had especially high hopes for this one.

Those of you in this group were carefree. Because you
could photosynthesize like plants, you had no need to eat,
and therefore had no sense of competition.

Yes, the thing that defined both of these groups was that
their need for conflict was almost nonexistent. In the plantlike group, the lack of conflict turned out to be a disadvan-
tage when it came to the group's survival.

While their lack of competition or conflict was admira-
ble, those of you in this group eventually lost even your desire
to compete to reproduce. As a result, your numbers started
on a slow but unrelenting downward spiral. The fewer of you
there were, the more plantlike you became, and in the end,

the majority of the individuals who remained lapsed into dormancy.

You know, I was really fond of them—the ones of you with greenish skin. They were friendly, but also respectful of one another, and most of all they had a great sense of humor. What's more, when they joked around, it was purely because they found things funny, not because they needed to release tension. There was a way in which they seemed to be amused by the very idea of being alive to begin with.

Maybe there are still a few of them left somewhere. Perhaps I could find them, if I tried. But they've already decided not to wake up. They were stubborn—now that they've chosen to go to sleep for the duration, you can trust they'll be true to their word.

If by some chance they should decide to open their eyes again, it will only be after the last of you have been eliminated from the face of the planet. They certainly had a sense of irony. If you asked them, though, I imagine they would describe it not as a prank, but just another cosmic joke.

I can almost see them now, waking from their slumber and peering around at a world without humans: they'll exclaim about the strangeness of it all, before turning to one another and sharing a hearty grin.

Now my story is finally nearing its end.

That's right, I still need to tell you about the other versions of me.

I've always said I have no personal preferences—or, to put it another way, I am not held to any set of values.

From the beginning, I wanted the me with personality to have a value system. That was how I'd be able to compare the differentiated me with the original, undifferentiated me, as I described previously, in order to determine whether it truly was *boring* to have no personality, as you believed.

It wasn't an easy task to create a version of me with personality. Even when I tried to imbue myself with qualities that might be considered to make up a personality, these things would soon become subsumed into my lack of individuation.

Every once in a while, though, a different me would be born. Specific genetic manipulations, specific techniques of bioengineering. At times, by chance, these would interact and succeed in producing an individual me.

You called her the great mother.

You clearly preferred her—the great mother, the one who had personality—over me.

When you grew up and left me to work as watchers, I rarely saw you display sadness or regret. When you left the great mother, you seemed distraught.

When you cried as infants, the great mother tenderly wiped away your tears with her spoonlike fingertips.

As juveniles, you ran home to the great mother, eager to tell her what had happened in your days, tripping over your words in your excitement, and the great mother smiled and stroked your hair tenderly.

Even as you approached maturity, you continued to seek

out the great mother, embracing her and pressing your soft cheeks against her body as you expressed your affection.

Physically, the great mothers were unstable. Their life spans were short, in some cases not even exceeding a hundred years. When one died, it would upset you so much that at one point I endeavored to increase the number of great mothers purely for this reason.

But I was unsuccessful.

Great mothers were vanishingly rare.

Truth be told, I could have worked a little harder to produce them—copies of myself that were, nonetheless, not me.

But having created the great mothers and compared myself to them, I didn't see myself as being inferior in any way.

I was not *boring*. At the same time, neither were the great mothers. Both were me. The only thing the great mothers had that I did not was a modicum of individuation. The great mothers were individual, while I was universal. That was all.

Granted, you found the great mothers almost irresistible.

According to my analyses, though, that was only because they shared more in common with you.

In short, you liked things that were similar to yourselves. What was different you rejected or, if not, discounted. You disowned your emotions toward that which was alien.

The great mother was simply another example of this tendency in you.

I'm sure the great mother will eventually be instrumental in some new development. It may not do much for you or for me. But the scale of something is hardly correlated to its importance. All of the things that have happened on Earth so far started out very small at first.

No, I never was too invested in creating great mothers. And yet, having produced them by chance, I think they have turned out to be a good thing.

This has been a long story—longer than it might have been, perhaps—but it seems we've almost reached its end.

I miss you all very much. I think fondly of how I was when I was with you.

I remember each and every one of you who called me Mother.

These memories are beautiful. Due to the absence of intentionality within me, I have never apprehended the value you called beauty. And yet I'm certain it's the word you would use to describe my memories of you:

Beautiful.

I have now arrived at a certain decision, which I expect you will hear more about in the next story.

\ Are You There, God? \

I wish I could be a human, Eli says.

"But you are," the great mother says with a smile.

"No." Eli pouts. "When you're a human you're not alone, like us. There's lots and lots of them, and they have families, and wars, and, um, love each other, and tons of other things. I can't do any of that."

"Oh, Eli," the great mother says warmly. "You and Lama are a family. You love each other, and you fight plenty."

"I don't just mean pretend like that. I want to have a real family, and real wars."

Lama, who has been listening quietly to Eli and the great mother's conversation, pipes up. "It wouldn't be as fun as you think."

"Why not?" Eli says, annoyed.

"It's supposed be hard, and hurt. War, and love, and all that stuff."

"Is that true?" Wide-eyed, Eli turns to the great mother.

With another smile, she says, "In a way," and shrugs. Lama leaves the room. She knows the conversation will go on for a while once Eli gets on this subject. The great mother puts the kettle on to boil. "Why don't we have some tea while we talk about this?" she says, warming two cups with hot water.

It's so warm here, Lama thinks.

The entrance to the house has an earthen floor and opens to the space with the kitchen and the big table where they eat. Eli's and Lama's rooms are to one side, and the great mother's is at the back. The corridor is just wide enough for two of them to pass each other, and the ceiling is comfortably low.

The window in Lama's room faces the sunrise. Eli's is opposite, where the sun sets. Outside their windows, plants grow thick. Birds clamor among the leaves. The occasional howl of a wandering large mammal strikes fear into Lama, but inside the house they're safe.

It's so cold outside. Lama loves bundling up in warm layers and going walking out in the forest with the great mother. She never goes alone, though. The outside is full of dangers.

Eli and Lama are twelve. They live with the great mother, who made them and takes care of them.

On their seventh birthday, the great mother had told them that they were the only humans left. Then, with a smile, she'd added, "And since you're the same sex, you can't even breed. How peaceful."

Lama was the first to ask, "Where do we go when we die?"

The great mother was slightly surprised. Eli was the one who always asked why. Lama usually kept quiet, listening in on Eli's questions and the great mother's responses without saying much.

"When things die, they rot and break down until their molecules and atoms go back into circulation around the physical world."

"I know all of that. What I want to know is, if I die, where do the thoughts that I'm thinking right now go?"

"Oh. Your thoughts are in your brain, so when your brain decomposes, they just disappear," the great mother said.

Lama thought about this for a moment.

"So all the thoughts of the humans who lived many, many years ago are gone?"

"That's right."

"Even though they used to be here?"

"That's right."

Lama breathed out with a *huff*. Then she gazed around at nothing in particular, as though there was something invisible in the room with them.

"What are you looking like that for?" Eli asked.

"Just checking in case there are any leftover thoughts floating around," Lama said.

Eli snorted. "Of course there aren't."

Lama sighed again.

"Were there really loads and loads of humans?"

Eli again. She, of course, was the one with a million questions.

"That's right," the great mother said kindly.

"Then why aren't there any left?"

"It's a long story."

"I don't care how long it takes."

"Well, I don't care for long stories, so I'll make it short."

"Come on! That's not fair."

"Humans went extinct."

"Then how come me and Lama are still here?"

"For succor, I suppose."

"Succor?"

"Perhaps you could call it consolation."

"I don't get it," says Eli, frustrated. "What do you mean?"

Eli's so impatient, Lama thinks. If only she wasn't so impatient, she might be able to sense the Presence, too.

Lama first noticed the Presence maybe a year after they turned seven and the great mother told them there were no other humans left.

"Hi, how are you?" the Presence said to Lama one day.

Of course, the Presence didn't talk to Lama in real words, so to be more precise it simply felt like the air right next to her trembled a little and then expanded—but anyway.

"Who said that?"

Lama spun around, but there was no one there. No one apart from Lama, Eli, and the great mother.

At first she thought an animal must have snuck inside the house. That first time, the Presence left almost immediately. But Lama sensed it again a few days later.

"Is it cold today? Or is it nice and warm?" the Presence asked Lama.

"It's warm in here. But it's always cold outside," Lama told the Presence. She was alone in her room, without the great mother, or Eli, or any roving animals. That was how Lama knew there was definitely someone there. And it was addressing her, Lama, personally.

Lama didn't feel scared of the Presence. On the contrary, she felt close to it in a way that she'd never felt with Eli or the great mother.

"Who are you?" Lama asked the Presence.

"Who am I?" the Presence answered. "Who am I? I don't know. I'm nobody, me."

Lama decided the Presence was a man. She had never seen a man, and didn't know what they were like, but still. Since the Presence was neither Lama, nor Eli, nor the great mother, what else could it be?

"See you later," Lama told the Presence, and left her room. The Presence followed Lama for a bit and then disappeared.

—

Eli enjoyed spending time with the great mother. It was fun to pester her and make her mad. When Eli was with the great mother, that was when she would laugh for joy, or cry for sorrow.

One day, Eli asked the great mother:

"Can I bring a bird here?"

This was right around the time that Lama started being able to sense the Presence.

The great mother said, "To do what with?"

"To spend time with it," Eli said.

"Oh, like a pet."

"A pet?" Eli didn't know what that was. The great mother often used words Eli didn't understand the meaning of. That was fun for Eli, too.

Eli brought a songbird with blue-gray wings back from the forest.

"I found it in the trap," she explained to Lama, excitedly.

Lama just nodded. She couldn't muster up too much interest in things like birds.

Eli let the bird loose inside the house. It took to the air and flew up toward the ceiling, beating its wings loudly, stopped on a shelf, circled the room, landed on the dining table, took off again, alighted on the great mother's shoulder, then flew around some more before finally colliding with the glass in the window and plummeting to the floor.

"It's not moving," Eli said, gently taking the bird into her cupped hands and peering at it with concern.

"Perhaps it's dead," the great mother said, and touched the bird. Its eyes blinked open, and it stirred in Eli's palm.

Without warning, it flapped its wings violently in an attempt to take flight. But its wing was broken, and it went nowhere.

"I should never have brought it inside," Eli said in tears.

"That's okay, it'll get better," the great mother said, taking the bird from her. The bird died that night, but the great mother kept that secret from Eli. Using the bird's cells, the great mother rapidly generated an accelerated clone that resulted three days later in a brand-new chick. She took it to Eli.

"What is this?" Eli said in surprise.

"It'll be a bird very soon," the great mother said, and showed Eli how to care for it. Eli raised the chick, which bonded with her and followed her around. It never crashed into the windows or scrambled around the room trying to find a way out.

Eli asked, "What happened to the bird I brought back?" but the great mother never gave her an answer.

Even now that she and Lama had turned twelve, the bird was devoted to Eli.

A few years ago she'd asked Lama, in a hushed tone, as though it were a grave revelation:

"The bird died, didn't it?"

Lama had nodded without saying anything.

Wasn't that obvious the whole time?

Back when it happened, the Presence had explained it to her:

(That bird's going to die soon. Then it'll join us on this side.)

–

The great mother sometimes told them stories about humans.

Lama never seemed that interested, but Eli was always desperate to find out more about them.

"Tell us the story of how the humans finally went extinct," she'd plead.

"What, again?" the great mother would say, amused.

And Eli would nod and say, "Yes, again."

Slowly, the great mother started the story:

All right. Well, the humans died out. It was always going to be a matter of time, of course, before they went extinct. But the mothers were delaying the inevitable. The mothers and the humans lived in symbiosis, of a kind. Once the humans were gone, the mothers would lose their reason to exist.

The humans kept doing the same things: loving one another, hating one another, fighting one another . . . You'd think they might have come up with something else to try, but no matter how many times they went around, they couldn't seem to change course.

Eventually the mothers got tired of it.

Let's wrap this up, they said. And they decided it would be the end.

"Were the mothers like you?"

"Yes, they were. Although not exactly."

"What was different about them?"

"They were much more impartial."

"Impartial!"

Another new word for Eli. She giggled in delight.

The mothers had made up their minds. That was enough—humans couldn't change. The mothers had been waiting on the possibility that humanity would transform, someday, but in the end it just never happened. It took a long time from when humanity was first born for it to die out. Hundreds of thousands of years. Maybe that wasn't so long for the life span of a species, but if it wasn't for the mothers, it would have been even shorter.

The sun was shining that day—the day that the mothers chose to be their last.

"The sun shone, the birds sang, the breeze blew, and the trees were laden with fruit," Eli added, her eyes bright. They were coming up to her favorite part of the story about how humanity met its end.

That's right. It was a sunny, pleasant day. The mothers had gradually been making preparations. They'd hidden themselves away, stopped creating watchers, and abandoned the human communities to fend for themselves. Without the discreet intervention of the watchers, it didn't take long for the groups to collapse. There were only a handful of humans left by the time of the final impact event.

"Did the humans keep loving and hating one another, even up to the end?"

"That's right. They were constant; almost admirably so, all the way until the end."

"Even as they went extinct, they were still loving and hating?"

"Yes, just like they used to before they ever started their decline—each one loving and hating right up to their last breath."

"Am I going to die, too?"

"You are, Eli."

The great mother continued:

Sometime after the last humans died, the mothers followed. There were several dozen mothers around the planet, but their awareness was linked. That was how they were able to coordinate. The mothers executed a thorough plan to destroy their own bodies. They swallowed tiny bombs with timed fuses so they would all explode in sync and burn away into nothing.

All the mothers in their different sectors exploded at the very same time. I watched it on the feed from the last remaining satellite orbiting Earth. The mothers swallowed the bombs before sunset, but by the time they went off, the hemisphere across which they were scattered was already plunged into night.

Earth gets dark at night. When the humans were still around, you could see their settlements lit up after the sun went down, but after they were gone, the faint glow of the mothers' lanterns was the only illumination on the planet. The stars and the moon shone so brightly through the night.

The mothers exploded and burned up like flowers opening and then falling to the ground. In the pitch dark, so many white flowers burst into bloom before quickly disappearing again.

I didn't see the images until the following day, so at the time that the explosion happened I heard only the sound of the nearest mother exploding in the distance. It made a much smaller sound than I'd been expecting. It was a nondescript, gentle *pop*.

"What was it like?" Eli asked.

"The sound?" The great mother considered for a while. "It wasn't like any other sound I've ever heard."

"Did you ever think about exploding together with the mothers?"

"I didn't."

"Why?"

"Maybe because . . ." The great mother trailed off into thought.

"Because what?"

"Maybe because I still had hope."

"Hope!"

Another word Eli didn't understand. She knew what it was supposed to mean, but she didn't really get it.

This time, the great mother didn't say anything.

She simply made the sound of the explosion again, finishing up the story of when the humans went extinct.

"Pop . . ."

For Lama, the Presence was the closest thing she had to a Friend. Lama had no friends, of course. Eli was Eli, and the great mother was the great mother.

The Presence taught Lama many things.

For instance, the idea of traveling, which Lama had never grasped.

(I used to be a traveler, once.)

It was snowing the day the Presence told her this. It was unusual for it to snow. The cold was always bitter, but the climate was dry where they lived, and they were far from the mountains.

(What's it like to travel?)

(You know, it was kind of like dreaming.)

Lama knew dreams. She dreamed in pretty colors. Eli's dreams were monochrome.

(I can never remember my dreams properly), Lama said, and she felt the Presence expand and surround her.

(That's it. That's what traveling feels like once it's over.)

That was how Lama learned that traveling was a little like dreaming.

She didn't know about singing, either. Neither the great mother nor Eli ever sang.

The Presence taught her a lullaby. Lama practiced it over and over, doing her best to imitate the Presence. When she'd learned it by heart, she sang it to Eli and the great mother, who were both very impressed.

The great mother said, "Of course—I'd forgotten about music. Lama, Eli, you must both start singing as much as you can." Then she burst into song on the spot. Unlike the Presence's faint melodies, the great mother's tune was bold.

(I like your song better), Lama thought, but really, any song was as invigorating as a clean breeze.

From then on, Lama and Eli sang every day.

"Are there really truly no more humans, aside from me and Lama?"

(There she goes again.) Lama made a face at the Presence.

In the beginning, the Presence had appeared only when Lama was on her own, but at some point it started to accompany her almost all the time. Once in a while she'd lose track of it, which made her feel strangely alone.

The great mother replied, "What makes you ask such a thing?"

"No answering a question with another question," said Eli.

"My, my, haven't you gotten clever, Eli."

"And no dodging!"

The great mother took a long look at Eli, then another at Lama, who appeared to be paying no attention at all. Then she said, "I'll tell you soon."

"You mean there are still humans somewhere after all!"

"What makes you think that?"

"Because you're always saying that humans went extinct. But when I ask you whether there are any humans left, you won't say. If there weren't any, you'd just say so."

"My, my, Eli, you really have grown."

"Like I said!" Eli huffed, and the great mother laughed. But Eli was enjoying herself.

Lama watched Eli's expression closely. Silently, she asked the Presence:

(Is it because Eli can't sense you that she has all these emotions? Because she needs them to talk to herself instead of talking to you?)

(I don't think so. You have a lot of different emotions, too.)

Did she? Lama tried to think.

(My heart just isn't as sensitive as Eli's.)

(That's not true.)

(But I'm not like her.)

(Of course you aren't. But the subtle ways your heart moves are just as real.)

(Do you feel emotions?)

(Sure I do. I was human, too.)

(Wait, you used to be human?) Lama was astonished. For some reason, she'd assumed the Presence was a kind of buildup of different things that drifted here and there throughout the world—not anything as definite as a human.

(I'm something else now. But a long time ago, I had a body and walked on the earth.)

(When was that?)

(Oh, I forget.)

Then the Presence asked brightly:

(How's humanity doing, by the way?)

Lama was surprised again. Didn't the Presence know?

"Humans went extinct," she blurted out loud, without meaning to. The great mother and Eli looked at her.

(Oh, really?) The Presence seemed unfazed.

"That's right. They went extinct, poor things," the great mother said. Like the Presence, she didn't seem all that troubled by it.

"So it's a bad thing to go extinct?" Eli said, pouncing on the answer.

Lama quickly said to the Presence again:

(What do you think? Do you think they're really all gone?)

The Presence said, with a hint of laughter:

(Sure, who knows? Why don't you ask the great mother like Eli always does?)

Lama turned to look at the great mother, only to find the great mother looking steadily at her.

For the first time, Lama let herself wonder if it could really be true:

Were there other humans out there somewhere? More of them than just her and Eli?

She felt a huge shiver run through her body.

There was something Eli had always wanted to ask the great mother.

She wanted to know about the person to whom the cells from which she'd been cloned had belonged.

This was a question that had always been close to Eli's heart. Over the years, whenever she encountered something that moved her, she would reach for the question and give it a nudge, then enjoy the way it rolled and wobbled. Eli took pleasure in savoring this mystery inside her almost as if it were a piece of hard candy in a cherished flavor. That was why, uncharacteristically, she'd kept it to herself all this time, without putting it to the great mother directly.

Eli and Lama turned eighteen.

"We'll celebrate," the great mother said.

They always had a few more dishes for dinner on their birthdays, but Lama wondered why this one was different.

The Presence told her:

(It's because you're a woman now.)

But—, Lama thought. *I've been grown for a while. Physically and mentally.*

"Is it special to turn eighteen?" Eli asked the great mother.

"A long time ago, and for a relatively long time, many societies regarded eighteen as the start of adulthood," the great mother said.

Eli thought this was her chance. Now that she was an adult, she should be able to ask about her origins.

"I need to ask you something," she said.

"What would that be?"

The great mother looked squarely at Eli. Lama had the feeling the great mother already knew what Eli was about to say.

"Where do I come from?"

"Come from?"

"The original me. What was she like?"

The great mother looked at her again. "She was called Rien."

"Rien?"

"Yes, Rien. She loved the great mother. And she lived true to her own will. Rien was never supposed to reproduce, but she had many children before she died. The great mother in her time gave the girls that were descended from her the same name. They all took after her very well."

"The great mother in her time?" Lama couldn't help but butt in.

"A great mother is born very rarely. When she dies, it's a long time before another one is eventually born."

This time it was Eli who asked, "Are you the same great mother as the great mother in Rien's time?"

The great mother shook her head. "No, I'm not. But our differences are insignificant. And of course, I have access to all of our memories."

"Rien . . ." Eli murmured the name the great mother had said. She rolled it around her mouth, much as she had poked and prodded the question inside her mind for so long.

"Did you like her, Great Mother?" Eli asked.

"Oh yes, I adored her. She was an active, curious, soft child," the great mother said with fondness in her voice.

To celebrate their birthday, the great mother gave Eli and Lama a book each.

What a beautiful thing a book is, Lama thought. The book the great mother gave to her was bound in leather, with pages that were rich in illustrations and gave off a marvelous smell.

Up until now, Lama had seen words and diagrams only on a screen, and those were wonderful, but nothing compared with the sensation of turning over the pages of a real book.

While Lama was bewitched by the material and texture of her book, Eli was quickly hooked by the content of hers.

"This tells you how to generate humans . . . So if I follow this recipe, I can meet them?" she asked, her excitement obvious.

"Meet them? That's a funny way of putting it. But I suppose so," the great mother said nonchalantly.

"Then I'm going to try it."

"It's an extremely difficult process."

"I don't care how long it takes."

Eli's eyes were shining. Lama wondered why Eli wanted to meet humans so badly. At the same time, she was heartened by the waves of energy she could feel radiating from Eli, her curiosity and ambition.

(Humans were probably more like Eli than they were like me), Lama mused. She pictured so many Elis milling around the place, chasing after one another, getting into spats. The idea pleased her.

Quickly a year passed, then another. On their twentieth birthday, uncharacteristically discouraged, Eli said, "Why isn't it working? Why can't I make a human?"

Lama paused, holding her sewing needle, and thought for a second. Then she took the needle and pressed it smoothly into the pad of her first finger. A red drop formed on her long, narrow fingertip.

"Look. Even a drop of blood is made up of dozens of different substances. Plus, its makeup changes in response to the state of the organism. An entire human has to be so many times more complicated than that," Lama said, trying to console Eli. She sucked on her finger.

Eli sighed. "You're right. Living things are complicated. I can't even build a single cell yet. Maybe there's no way I'll ever create a human."

"The great mother must know how, though," Lama said.

Eli nodded bitterly. "Of course. She made us, after all."

After that, Eli stopped trying to make humans. Instead, she started going outside all the time. It was cold outside, and the forest was dark and deep, but that didn't seem to bother her in the least.

Carrying her camping gear in her pack, Eli wandered through the forest for weeks at a time. Lama got worried and went to talk to the great mother about it, but the great mother only shook her head equably.

"Let her be," she said. "That's just the way Eli is. When that child puts her mind to something, there's no talking her out of it."

But the great mother's words filled Lama with an unease she couldn't place.

(Why does Eli always have to feel so strongly about everything?)

Lama had no desire to go outside. She wanted to stay in with the Presence where it was warm. She wanted to sew and cook, read words and look at graphics, clean the house and put up preserves, and when night fell to gaze out her window into the darkness before crawling under the covers and sinking into technicolor dreams.

Every night as she drifted off, Lama wondered whether Eli was looking for humans out there.

Neither Eli nor the great mother ever appeared in Lama's dreams.

After spending time outside, Eli always returned a little thinner.

One day, she came back and held out something grayish toward Lama and the great mother.

"It's for you."

Lama took it gingerly. She'd never seen anything like it before.

"Bone—mammalian," the great mother said.

"This is a bone?" asked Lama.

Eli and the great mother both nodded.

"How do you not know what bones look like, Lama? There are pictures in your book," Eli said, raising her eyebrows.

Lama tried to recall. All the illustrations in her book were beautiful, but they didn't seem real. Compared with the bright, dimensional graphics she was used to seeing on a screen, they were as round-edged and pleasant as scenes from her dreams.

"I just didn't know they were so small."

"This is only a part. A tiny piece."

Lama closed her hand over the bone. It felt brittle, as if the slightest pressure would make it crumble.

"Are my bones this flimsy, too?" she asked the great mother.

"No, this mammal must have died quite some time ago. The bone will have been weathered over time by the wind and the rain."

"There's no chance it's human, is there?" Eli said quietly.

"Of course not," said the great mother.

Eli took out a transparent bag from her backpack. It was maybe a third full with a gritty, powdery material that seemed to be remnants of bone.

"This is a mix of bone from all different mammals. And

some of it's probably just sand. The piece I gave you was the best one I found."

Lama took another look at the bone Eli had given them. It was flat and thin, with just the hint of a curve to it.

"Thanks. It's beautiful," she said, sincerely.

Lama had a recurring dream.

The first time she had it wasn't long after the Presence first appeared, before she turned ten.

At first there was nothing—just a flat area of land, with a few plantlike things growing on it. The sun cast a harsh glare from close overhead. Lama stepped forward cautiously onto dry, cracked soil. There wasn't enough room to walk around, so she just stood there.

The small piece of land was surrounded by water. Things were moving in this water—some very small, some as big as her.

This dream was the only dream in which she noticed whether it was hot or cold or how the air smelled.

Lama found herself floating in the dream's echoes even once she opened her eyes.

(I know that place), the Presence said, to Lama's surprise.

(Where is it?)

(I was there once.)

(Is that where you were born?)

(That's right, I was born there. And died there. And then was born again.)

Lama rubbed her eyes in confusion. Her brain wasn't

awake yet, and this was back before she learned a lot of what she knew now.

The dream appeared to her many times over the years. The limited land expanded, the water drew back, and she started to see the things that moved in it. Lama enjoyed these dreams.

It dawned on her several years later—when the great mother started to teach her and Eli about history—that what she was witnessing in her dreams might be the evolution of Earth.

Eli and Lama turned twenty-five. Eli had stopped going outside and rededicated herself to trying to create humans.

Neither the great mother nor Lama set foot in Eli's room anymore. It was impossible to avoid tripping over or disturbing something: Eli's jumbled collections of the equipment that she had cobbled together and the homebrew chemicals that she had concocted lay haphazardly over every surface, covering the floor and overflowing from her closet. The great mother's shape, in particular, made it impossible for her to move around the space without causing some kind of accident.

"Can't you clean up a little in there?" the great mother would grouse. Eli ignored her.

Year by year, time moved on. Each time she started work on a new round of experiments, Eli would hole up in her room for days, sometimes weeks at a time.

But where once she had been so adamant about how much she longed to meet humans, at some point she'd stopped talking about it.

Lama asked the great mother why she refused to make more humans now.

"I can't bear to watch them grow only to fail again."

"Hm . . ."

Lama wasn't sure what to say to that.

Were humans so doomed to always go extinct?

(Human or not, everything dies eventually), the Presence said in Lama's ear.

(Hmm . . .)

Lama made another noncommittal sound.

"Eli! What is that?" Lama heard the great mother shout one day. It was unlike the great mother to be so loud.

"This? Nothing much. Just a primitive eukaryote," Eli responded, holding a glass vial. It contained a small brown lump. On closer inspection, Lama saw the lump was quivering.

"It's moving," the great mother said, peering at it.

"Because it's a collective," Eli said, handing her the vial. "By themselves, they're barely multicellular."

The great mother took the vial from Eli and studied the lump.

"Where did you find this?"

"Nowhere. I made it."

"You did?"

"Yep. Of course, it was built from an original sample."

"And where did you get those cells?"

"From me."

The great mother moved her gaze from the vial to Eli. She looked at her almost as hard as she'd looked at the brown lump.

"You invented the method yourself?"

"It's hardly an invention. The book you gave me explained clonogenesis pretty thoroughly."

"But this isn't a clone of you."

"No, I haven't been able to make cloning work. Although I've figured out how to turn my cells into other organisms."

Eli seemed dissatisfied. The lump in the vial was still quivering.

(I've seen something like this before—in a dream), Lama thought.

Yes. It was a dream she'd had when she was maybe fifteen. In this dream, fauna were just starting to move out of the water. Plants had already started colonizing the land. The animals crossed the border between sea and land uncertainly: fishlike things, huge mollusks, things that slithered and dragged. Among them floated strange-looking clumps, light green, pale red, or brownish. Some stayed in the water, while others slowly inched their way up the shore.

Those lumps had stopped appearing in her dreams not long afterward.

She'd wondered then whether successive waves of change had overtaken them.

"It's adorable," Lama said, carefully cradling the vial the great mother handed her.

"Yep. It's a cutie," Eli said with a grin. Lama smiled back.

On their thirtieth birthday, Eli created a bird.

"This is my birthday present," she said, holding it out in her hands.

"And here I thought presents were supposed to be for the one having the birthday," the great mother laughed, taking the bird.

"This one's for you, Lama," Eli went on, giving her a small blue-gray bird. It looked just like the one Eli had brought home years ago—the one that had flown into a window and died.

"Are you still working on humans?"

"No luck so far. I'm using my own cells, so you'd think it would be easier to use the clonal technique, but it just doesn't seem to take."

"Are you using a different method than the one in the book? Something you came up with on your own?"

"Yep. I've tried over and over, but it kept going wrong using the method in the book. Maybe I just don't have the touch for it."

"But that's wonderful," the great mother exclaimed. "To do something you haven't been shown and come up with something new—it's quite remarkable."

The great mother stroked Eli's head.

"You used to do this all the time when I was little," Eli said bashfully, before ducking and moving away from her.

"What should I do with this?" Lama said.

Laughing, Eli said, "You should keep it."

"I don't think I can do that."

"Of course you can."

"I'm too scared."

So Lama refused to take the bird. The great mother took both birds and cared for them, feeding and watering them every morning and night. At first the birds were only small, but they grew and grew until they looked nothing like the bird Eli had once wanted to keep. Soon the two birds— which, for whatever reason, none of them had ever thought to name—started to talk, just a little:

"How did you sleep?"

"See you in the morning."

"The snow's coming down."

That was the kind of thing the birds would say.

"Are they copying the sounds they hear us making?" Lama wondered.

The great mother shook her head. "I think they know what the words mean."

(Well, I've never seen anything like it), said the Presence, suspiciously. (I'm telling you, there's something odd about them.)

The Presence gave the birds a wide berth.

Time moved forward in Lama's dream. Flora and fauna flourished on dry land, and a *Homo sapiens*-like species emerged.

These mammals were taller than Lama. They had thick hair on their bodies, and the scraps of cloth they wore barely covered any of their well-developed muscles.

"Are you a human?" Lama asked the animal in her dream.

The animal looked at her with curiosity. Her words seemed to mean nothing to it. She didn't know whether the animals even had language. But it had a scent—a peculiar scent she didn't recognize.

Lama said to the animal, "Something tells me Eli might like the way you smell," before trying to hurry out of the dream. The animal stepped toward her. It reached for her arm. Lama screamed. Undeterred, the animal grabbed her. Its grip was impossibly strong. Just in the nick of time, she woke up.

(It almost got me), Lama told the Presence.

(Oh, really?) the Presence replied airily. (But how else are you going to meet a man?)

The Presence sounded amused.

(A man?) Lama said, startled. (That was a man?)

It was much bigger than she'd imagined, and gave off far more heat, and seemed much more dangerous. Did breeding really involve dealing with one of those?

(No thanks, not for me), Lama said with a shudder.

(Men aren't so bad), the Presence said, even more amused now.

Lama shook her head again.

In the next dream, *Homo sapiens* already dominated the ecosystem, and Lama observed the entire group of them from higher ground. The humans paid no attention to anything but themselves, and paid no attention to Lama, which meant she was spared another direct encounter. She breathed a sigh of relief.

In the dream after that one, Lama was even higher up. The humans were making all kinds of noise.

(What are all these voices?) she wondered.

When she woke up, the Presence said:

(Oh, those were prayers.)

In the next dream, and the next, the humans kept praying. Save me . . . Help me . . . Give me . . . Make it . . . Smite them . . . From the simple to the involved, they bombarded Lama with all manner of wishes and requests.

Lama started waking up from her dreams drenched in sweat.

(I don't like humans), she complained to the Presence.

The Presence laughed. (Aren't you a human, too?)

Which would be easier, Lama wondered: to go down to where the humans were and breed with a man, or to stay high up and keep having to listen to their prayers? She didn't feel inclined to do either, if she had a say in it.

The spring that she and Lama turned thirty-seven, Eli finally succeeded in creating a human.

"You did it! What an achievement!" The great mother lavished her with praise. Lama felt slightly jealous.

(And that human is so small. Even smaller than the bird), she thought to herself, but she kept quiet because she didn't want them to think she was saying it only out of spite.

The human had fair skin and dark hair and dark eyes. Of course, it couldn't walk yet, since it had just been born. It lay on its back in Eli's palm, wriggling.

"Your human . . . It's on the small side," Lama said, choosing her words carefully.

"Uh huh. It isn't even a real human. It's just a look-alike."

"A look-alike?"

"Yep. I kept trying to make a clone from my own cells, but it just didn't work. So I had to use mouse cells and manipulate the genetics until I could make them express a human form. So it looks like a human, but the cells and genes are from a different species."

"Huh."

Lama didn't really get it. No, she understood what Eli was saying easily enough. But she didn't know why Eli was so determined to create humans to begin with.

(All they do is ask for things), she thought.

Beside her, the Presence said nothing.

In Lama's dream, she seemed to be the humans' god.

She knew about gods, in theory. Human societies had various forms of worship, and since these conceptions of divinity were deeply implicated in the psychological structures of individuals as formed by their respective societies, differences of religion were often the root of conflict . . . and so on.

Waking from her latest dream, Lama complained:

(What do they even want a god for?)

She couldn't stand how the humans in her dream cast

all their hopes and fears on her, idolizing her as some kind
of deity.

(They're terrified of dying), the Presence explained.

(That's it?)

(Aren't you?) the Presence asked Lama.

Lama took a moment to think. The thought of herself
dying didn't really bother her at all. She was more afraid of
Eli or the great mother dying—but even then it was more
displeasure that she felt, rather than fear.

(It doesn't mean that much to you), the Presence said.

(What doesn't?)

(Life.)

"Of course it does," Lama said out loud.

She didn't want to die. It just didn't scare her.

Among the humans, there were plenty who didn't pray at
all. Maybe they weren't afraid of dying, either. But no—that
didn't seem to be it.

"Humans make no sense," Lama said again.

The Presence agreed. (You're right, humans make no
sense at all. You included.)

Lama remembered the Presence saying something like
this before.

As if to herself, she said:

(Do you think Eli's humans ever pray?)

The Presence didn't reply.

Eli built a town. It had a river running through it. Its
streets were lined with small houses inhabited by the small

look-alike humans she'd created. At the edge of the town was a factory, which made more humans using Eli's own methods. The same factory also produced the small animals that the humans used for food.

The look-alike humans lived peacefully. They formed bonded pairs, but because of the factory they didn't reproduce, instead raising the small children that were created in the factory from cells derived from various other species.

It took something like a hundred and fifty years for the town to find its stride. Eli and Lama were coming up to their two hundredth birthday. Time in the town passed peacefully.

At some point Lama had asked Eli, "Did you have a reference for the town?"

"I borrowed the trappings of a certain historical period in a country I've always liked, but there was never an actual place like this. I doubt humans could have built such a calm, quiet community," Eli had replied evenly. Both she and Lama had grown much older, but they didn't seem to be at all close to dying yet.

The town's inhabitants lived out their lives. Maybe once every ten years or so, there would be a pair of small humans who decided they wanted to seek a different life, or small animals that decided they wanted to avoid being slaughtered. They went down the river and out of the town.

"Where do they go after they leave?" Lama asks Eli.

"They seem to form their own settlements. If they survive, they establish a new way of living."

"They aren't human, though. Not really?" Lama says with a smile.

But Eli looks serious. "Whatever they are, if they make it and start a new society, that's all I can ask."

"If you say so." This time Lama chuckles, thinking of the town full of small ersatz humans. The look-alikes don't worship a god. They have no interest in gods or myths.

Come to think of it, the humans in Lama's dream that used to worship her had died out some time ago—when she was a hundred and fifty, or thereabouts.

"O Lord, why hast thou, O Lord?"

During the long years it took for them to go extinct, so many of them had perished with the same question on their lips, not once doubting that humanity would someday recover and be redeemed.

Lama had never felt sympathetic to any of their pleas, except one. A small child, who had dying asked:

"Are you there, God?"

For whatever reason, the child's prayer had touched her.

(Maybe because she reminded me of me), Lama thinks.

It was true, the child was just like Lama had been when she was a girl. From the way she moved, to her voice, to her smell.

The child went on praying quietly. She did it without much hope, but she poured herself into it nonetheless. The child didn't even look like she was praying. In spite of that, every moment she was alive, she was asking:

Are you there, God? Why is this happening to us?

Lama found herself moved to prayer for the first time in her life.

(Oh you . . . dear humans . . . won't you find some way to help one another?)

(I hope someone's listening), the Presence said.

(It's too late anyway. There are no humans left to hear me.)

(No, it's okay. They're always here. Over here with me.)

Can that be true, Lama wonders. Are you really all over there? And if you are, what are you doing there?

When Lama dreams now, there is only a wild, windswept moor.

(When do you think it'll be my time to die?) Lama asks the Presence.

(Who knows? You and Eli seem to have really long lives. If you die, though, you can come over and join us on this side.)

(What's it like there?)

(Here? Everything exists, but nothing changes.)

Lama thinks again of the town that Eli made. The small new people bathe in the river that runs through it. The women and children don light gauzy robes and file down the flagstone path to the water. Sometimes, two of them will take a boat and sail downstream, to reach a new place where they can start a new story. How will that story go? Who will tell it, and whom will they tell it to?

(These new humans don't know what they've got), the Presence sometimes says, sulkily.

Lama just smiles. It's warm where she is. So very warm. And the ceiling is comfortably low.

She remembers the girl. "Are you there, God?" she says under her breath, seeking some kind of solace, or comfort.

Try as she might, though, she can't think of anything to ask for.

So instead she prays for humanity, which went extinct many ages ago:

You humans. Who once were alive, just like me. May you find a way to save yourselves.

Day after day she sends out this quiet plea, without knowing whether or not there's anyone out there to hear it.

HIROMI KAWAKAMI was born in Tokyo in 1958. Her first novel, *Kamisama* (God), was published in 1994. In 1996, she was awarded the Akutagawa Prize for "Hebi o Fumu" ("Tread on a Snake"), and in 2001, she won the Tanizaki Prize for her novel *Sensei no Kaban* (*Strange Weather in Tokyo*), which became an international bestseller. *Strange Weather in Tokyo* was short-listed for the 2013 Man Asian Literary Prize and the 2014 International Foreign Fiction Prize. Kawakami has contributed to editions of *Granta* in both the UK and Japan and is one of Japan's most popular contemporary novelists.

ASA YONEDA is the translator of Banana Yoshimoto's *Dead-End Memories*, *Moshi Moshi*, *The Premonition*, and *Mittens and Pity*, as well as *Idol, Burning* by Rin Usami and *The Lonesome Bodybuilder* by Yukiko Motoya.